CRYSTAL'S CRUSH

A SWEET 16 DIARIES NOVEL

BY

SPARKLE

Wahida Clark Presents Young Adult
60 Evergreen Place
Suite 904A
East Orange, New Jersey 07018
973-678-9982
www.wclarkpublishing.com
www.wcpyoungadult.com

Crystal's Crush
ISBN 13-digit 978-1936649426
ISBN 10-digit 1936649462
Library of Congress Catalog Number 2013910058
  1. Young Adult, Contemporary, Urban Fiction, African American, – Fiction
  2.
Cover design by Nuance Art nuanceart@gmail.com
Interior book design by Nuance Art nuanceart@gmail.com
www.acreativenuance.com

Printed in United States
Green & Company Printing and Publishing, LLC
www.greenandcompany.biz

ACKNOWLEDGMENTS

I thank God for His grace and mercy.

To my mother, my role model, who taught me the importance of family, I say thank you.

I would also like to thank Wahida Clark for again, giving me this opportunity. Thank you Dr. Maxine Thompson for hanging on in there with me.

I want to thank the parents, librarians, teachers and book clubs for sharing information about my previous book, Sade's Secret. I want to give a special shout out to K.C. Boyd, Jennifer Coissiere, Angelia Menchan and Shantal Young.

To my author friends who are there in the trenches with me, thank you.

Last, but not least, this book is dedicated to every teenager out there who has ever had a dream. Know that with faith and hard work, your dreams can come true. I'm living proof.

Sparkle

CHAPTER ONE
CRYSTAL

Dear Diary,
Where is the love? Love don't live here anymore; only drama.

Peace doesn't reside at 2658 Wilkinson Road. It hasn't lived here in over a year. The constant bickering between my parents, Kevin and Maddie Jackson, make me feel like I'm hanging out in a war zone. I would rather spend countless hours at school than at home. That's how bad things have gotten.

Enough about me and my problems. I can't imagine being sixteen and pregnant like my best friend, Sade Washington. I get confused on what to do to help her. What can I do for her when she's having a child by her stepfather? On top of that, she's dealing with Ms. Joyce, her mom, who didn't want to believe her. Yes, Sade has issues and my hand would cramp writing about all of them.

"Crystal, turn on the TV . . . hurry up!" Dena Bradford, my other best friend, said frantically as she entered my room without knocking and plopped down on my bed. Her long micro-braids covered her oval face. She took one hand and pulled them back.

I threw my diary to the side and picked up the remote. I wasn't moving fast enough for Dena. She snatched the remote and turned to one of the local Dallas news channels.

We watched as the news showed scenes from the hospital. People were holding on to each other and crying. Jamie Abbott, the reporter said, "We're back with updates on the shooting at Metro Hospital. Calvin Thomas, who was in police custody for having sex with a minor, was pronounced dead ten minutes ago. The child molester murdered his own baby. Police and hospital staff are baffled at the chain of events. No other casualties reported."

"Oh my God!" I kept saying over and over. "I can't believe this!"

Dena placed her hand on top of my arm. "Sade's frantic but alive. I talked to her mom and rushed over here to tell you."

I stood up and started looking for my shoes under my bed. "We need to get to the hospital. I have to make sure she's okay for myself."

About thirty minutes later, but it seemed more like a lifetime; we were on the bus headed toward the hospital.

The crowd had thinned from what I'd seen earlier on the news, but the police were still swarming around. We walked toward the emergency door exit. An officer blocked our entry. "Ladies, you will have to find another way into the hospital. This part is off limits."

"But my friend just had a baby. I wanted to check on her," I said.

"Young lady, find another door to enter." He placed his hand on his waist and continued to block the door.

Dena grabbed my arm. "Come on. I know another way in."

Dena and I rushed to the side of the hospital. We stopped at the front desk to find out Sade's room number.

"There's Ms. Joyce!" Dena said, waving her arms.

Ms. Joyce must have seen her because she walked over to where we stood. "Come with me, girls. Maybe you two can comfort Sade."

We followed Joyce to Sade's room. Sade's grief-filled, tear-stained face stared back at us. Dena and I rushed to her side. We held on tight to each other. Sade said over and over, "He killed my baby. He killed my baby."

When I thought of evil, Calvin's face appeared in my vision. Calvin was the monster who had been molesting Sade since she was nine years old.

"I still don't understand how he got to the baby. We didn't even get a chance to see her," Dena wailed.

"I can't believe this. I can't believe this," Sade said. "My baby is dead."

Ms. Joyce wiped the tears from her face with the tissue Dena handed her. My heart broke for my friend. It took me a minute to digest all Sade's mom had told us. Calvin slipped out of his handcuffs when the officer who was supposed to be guarding him went to the bathroom. Ms. Joyce didn't know how he got inside the nursery, but poor Little Unique never had a chance.

CHAPTER TWO
Ty

This is not the type of life I'd envisioned for myself. In fact, when I was a little boy, I thought I would be the next Emmitt Smith. The Cowboys were and still are my favorite team. Maybe my dreams of being an NFL player wouldn't have been killed if it wasn't for my dad deciding he didn't want a family anymore, and then leaving my mom alone to take care of me and my brother when I was only nine years old.

My older brother, Michael, got tired of seeing my mom cry every night, so he decided to help out by doing odd jobs that eventually led him into working for one of the most notorious drug dealers in the Dallas/Fort Worth area. I'd always looked up to my brother, so quite naturally I wanted to do whatever he did. Michael did everything he could to keep me out of "the life", but when his boss realized I was an athlete, he wanted to tap into that area. So here I am, supplying drugs to athletes all around the city. Instead of being the star player I knew I had the capability to become,

I was more widely known as Doughboy. My pockets stayed full. If you needed a hit, I was the go-to guy.

On this day, I was sitting in my souped-up silver Dodge Charger that my brother recently purchased for me, waiting on my friend JC to come out of his house. A white Camry pulled up, and a girl who I'd seen several times before exited.

JC entered the car. "Sorry it took me so long, man. I had to use the bathroom."

"Who is that girl?" I asked, pointing to the female in the tight jeans and Dallas Mavericks T-shirt. Her ponytail bounced from side to side as she walked up the stairs at the house across the street.

"That's Crystal. She's not your type. You don't want to mess with her, man. Besides, her dad ain't having that."

"Are y'all cool?" I asked, not trying to hear everything else JC was saying.

"Oh yeah. That's my girl. We've been friends since we moved over here. Other dudes have tried to talk to her, but she shuts them down. I'm just warning you. Besides, she's one of the good ones, and I don't want to see you hurt my friend."

"JC, I thought we were boys. What makes you think I'd hurt her?"

"Ty, it's me, man. You wrap it, slip in, and move on. Crystal's not the type of girl you screw over."

"Sounds like you got a crush on her or something. If you do, then I'll stop with the questions and move on," I said as I eased the car out on the street, taking one last glance in Crystal's direction. She seemed to turn and look my way. I wasn't sure if it was my imagination, but I swore a smile crossed her face right before she went in her house and closed the door.

"Naw, I don't like Crystal like that. She more like a play cousin or something. If you really want to holla at her, I'll see what I can do."

"For real? If you do that, I owe you one."

"You ain't said nothing but a word."

JC pulled out his cell phone, called a number, and hit the speaker button. "Crystal, it's me, JC. What's up with you?" he asked.

I felt guilty listening to what probably should have been a private conversation between Crystal and JC, as she told him about the dilemma with her friend Sade. I thought my life was filled with drama. Whoever this Sade chick was, had been dealt a bad hand. That's cold that she lost her baby to the same pervert who raped her.

JC hung up the phone. "Man, I'll talk to her another time. She's dealing with a lot right now."

"I can tell. No rush. I'm willing to wait as long as I need to for her."

"Man, you talking like you all in love and stuff."

I blew it off. "Love? Please! I ain't never even talked to the chick. I just want to get to know her. You know, see where it leads. Tired of being on these streets without a girl to call my own, you know?"

JC scrolled through his cell phone. "Man, I ain't trying to hear that. I'm trying to get with as many girls as I can get with."

"See, that's why your little pee wee is going to fall off. My brother told me I better find one good girl and leave those ratchets alone before I catch something I can't get rid of."

"He does have a point. I ain't trying to go out like no sucka."

"Let's find us some chicks to chill with," I said.

"Looks like you already found who you want. But it's so much candy out there, I don't know who I want to single out," JC said.

My cell phone beeped. It was an incoming text message from my older brother, Michael. For now, I had to push thoughts of Crystal out of my head. Time to handle business. I drove to the location left on the phone.

I pulled up in the driveway as instructed. Without getting out of my car, I rolled down the window and one of Michael's workers handed me what looked like an ordinary grocery bag. The bag contained a new supply of pills that I needed to deliver to one of the guys on another block.

I turned the radio up as one of my favorite songs played and eased back on the road.

JC said, "I think we're being followed."

I glanced in my rearview mirror. A gray Lincoln turned every time I turned. I hoped it wasn't five-o. Up until now I had avoided being on the police radar. I was only sixteen, but with Texas laws, I could still be tried as an adult for a drug offense, and I wasn't trying to have that.

Once I flipped a switch on my Charger, I sped away and didn't slow down until I knew the Lincoln was no longer in sight. I parked out of clear view. "I don't know who that was, but I got to be more careful," I said.

JC kept looking behind us. Sweat was streaming from the side of his face. "Man, I don't think that was five-o. That looked like some of Slick's boys."

My brother's boss? Why would his men be following me? I'm on the low end of the totem pole. I need to contact my brother to see if there was something I needed to know.

CHAPTER THREE
CRYSTAL

I cried as Unique Washington was laid to rest a week after being killed. Dena and I tried to shield Sade from members of the local media who repeatedly snapped photos as we left in a donated limousine, courtesy of the funeral home.

My mom decided to have the repast at our house, so the limousine dropped us off there. Under normal circumstances, we would have been excited to have our neighbors ooh and aah as we passed by, but with the solemn occasion, it irked me to see how nosy our neighbors were.

Sade barely said anything since leaving the hospital. The doctor had assured her mom that this was normal. I missed the old Sade. The one who would make me smile when I was feeling down. I didn't know what to say to her to get her to smile.

My mom and her friends swarmed around Joyce. Now don't get me wrong. Ms. Joyce was Sade's mom, and I respected her, but I still blamed her for bringing Calvin into their lives. If she had listened to Sade, maybe, just maybe, Sade wouldn't be going through all of this now.

"You need to eat something, dear," my mom said as she handed Sade a plate filled with chicken and potato salad.

Sade pushed the plate away. "No thanks, Ms. Maddie. I'm not hungry."

"Please. Eat something for me. If you don't eat it, I'll be forced to, and you know I can't stand to gain any more weight." Mom laughed, but Sade didn't.

"I'll make sure she eats it," I said.

Mom raised her eyebrow, but left Sade, Dena, and me alone on the front porch.

I made sure my mom was back in the house before talking. "Sade, you do need to eat something."

"My life is such a mess. Food's the last thing on my mind."

I placed my hand on Sade's and squeezed it. "You survived dealing with Calvin, and you will survive this too."

Sade looked at me and in a low shaky voice said, "He killed my baby."

I didn't know what to say. Instead, we all just sat on the porch in silence looking toward the street.

One of JC's friends pulled up in front of his driveway. I'd seen him before. I didn't know his name though. Dressed in jeans and a Dallas Cowboys jersey, he exited the car. From a distance, he looked to be several inches taller than me, and we were the same nutmeg brown complexion. Unlike some of the guys who liked to wear their hair long, his hair was cut close, so close he looked almost bald.

I didn't mean to get caught staring. He glanced our way and waved. I was busted, so I waved back. He smiled. I didn't. I didn't feel like I had anything to smile about. An SUV pulled up in front of my house, blocking the view to JC's house.

"Brandon!" Sade said. It was the first time she seemed to have some life. Before Brandon could make it up the walkway, Sade was in his arms.

Dena and I watched the exchange. We both were probably thinking the same thing. *Why wasn't Brandon at the funeral?* But we kept our comments to ourselves.

Sade's eyes seemed to light up, so I guess Brandon being here, even if at the last minute, wasn't all too bad. For a brief moment, she seemed to be back to her old self.

Brandon gave Dena and me a hug. "I'm glad you two were there for Sade."

"Where were you?" Dena blurted out.

Sade gave her a "don't go there" look. Out of respect for Sade, Dena backed down.

Sade led Brandon into the house. We followed them. Brandon was the only person who was able to get Sade to eat. A few hours later, all of my mom's friends were gone. I walked with Sade to the end of the driveway and watched her get in the car with Brandon.

JC's friend walked across the street. "Hey, can I talk to you for a moment?" he said.

I stood with my arms crossed. "I don't feel like talking. Maybe another time." I turned to walk back to the house.

"How do I reach you?" JC's friend asked.

"Ask JC. He has my number." I never turned around. Instead, I increased my pace and exhaled as soon as I closed the door. I peeked through the curtains. JC's friend was still staring at the house. I watched as he walked back up to JC's front door.

"Kevin, the least you can do is help me clean up with your lazy ass!" Maddie shouted.

Oh no, here we go again, I thought as the shouting match between my mom and dad went into full swing. Both of them had a little liquor in them, so this could go on for hours. The sad look on my ten-year-old sister's face mirrored mine. "Hey kid, you want to watch the *Princess Diaries*?"

Hope shrugged her shoulders. "Sure."

I turned the volume up on the television to drown out our parents arguing back and forth.

"I hate them!" Hope shouted.

"Don't say that. They are our parents. They are just going through a rough spot right now."

"Come on, Crystal. They've been fighting like this for months. All year. I really wish I had another set of parents." Hope was only voicing what I had been feeling lately, but with me being the older sister, I had to be the voice of reason.

"Adults fight. They still love us."

"Sure they do. Neither one of them couldn't care less what I have going on in my life. I got in trouble last week. I tried to talk to Dad about it, and he blew me off. I tried to talk to Mom, and she told me she would look at the note later. Well, later never came."

"Where's the paper they are supposed to sign? I'll sign it."

Hope left and went to her room. She soon returned with the slip of paper that stated that she was talking too much in class. I looked at her. "You know you shouldn't be talking in class, right?"

"Of course I do, but I was bored."

Now my parents had taken it too far. Their spats were affecting Hope. Something needed to be done about this.

CHAPTER FOUR
TY

At first, JC acted like he didn't want to give me shorty's number. I still think he had a little crush on her. Why else would he be tripping over giving me her number? I really didn't want it to be a problem between us, so hopefully he was telling me the truth.

I ran an errand for my brother and then settled down in our crib before dialing Crystal's number. The phone rang several times before I heard her soft, sexy voice on the other end.

"Did I catch you at a bad time?" I asked.

"It depends. Who is this?" she asked.

"The man of your dreams."

"I know this isn't Chris Brown, so who is this?" she asked again.

Glad to know she liked a little bad boy. "Tyreek Davis. But my friends call me Ty."

"Tyreek? I don't know a Tyreek. Do we go to school together or something?" she asked.

"I'm JC's friend."

"Oh, it's you." She sounded nonchalant.

"In the flesh. So now that you know who I am, maybe you'll let me come over one day."

"For what?"

"To see you. I really would like to get to know you better. See what's behind that pretty face of yours."

"I'll think about it."

"What can I do to convince you to change your mind?"

"Nothing. Besides, if you're serious you'll figure it out."

Without saying another word, Crystal hung up the phone. I didn't know what it was about her that made her different. Plenty of girls in my neighborhood would die at a chance to be my girl, but I just wasn't feeling them. Crystal had that something special, and I was determined to find out what it was.

I was daydreaming about Crystal when a bamming noise on the front door interrupted me. Easing my hand on my pistol, I got up to see who was outside. I didn't see anyone, so I went and sat back down on the sofa. Heard another bam on the door. Got up, looked outside again, and didn't see anything. This time I opened the door. Before I could get the door all the way open, I felt two hundred plus pounds ram into me. I hit the floor hard, bruising my backside. "What the . . ." I yelled.

"Doughboy, have you seen your brother?" one of the men dressed in all black asked. As soon as my eyes were no longer dazed, I recognized him as Pork. One of Slick's men. One of the dudes that worked with my brother.

The other man raised his hand and helped me up. I held my back and frowned. "Naw, man. I haven't talked to Michael since earlier. What's up?"

"Big Mike owes us some money, and we're just trying to collect," Pork said.

"You know he's good for it. So why y'all coming over here harassing me?" I asked, trying to sound all hard, although I was scared. If Slick was sending his men after Michael, my brother must have really screwed up something.

"Well, we know that. But he was supposed to be somewhere at three. It's five and being late is something that Slick don't play," Pork responded, looking down at me with his cold, piercing black eyes.

"If I talk to him, I'll tell him you looking for him. Next time, you don't have to be so rough on a brother."

"If there's a next time, we won't come a knocking. Guarantee that." Pork and his sidekick turned and walked out the house.

I sighed with relief the moment I saw the door close. I got strength and rushed to lock both locks on the door. I picked up my cell phone and dialed Michael's number. "Man, where are you?" I yelled.

"Chill out, lil' bro. I got a lot going on," he responded.

"Man, you almost got me killed."

"What are you talking about, Ty?"

"Pork and some other dude just came by here looking for you. The other dude bum rushed me. Tried to knock my back out."

"I forgot I was supposed to drop something off. Are you okay? They didn't hurt you, did they?"

"No, I'm fine. Just shook up a little."

"Lay low. I'll be by the crib later." Without another word, my brother hung up the phone.

I didn't know where his mind was, but it better be about Slick's business because he didn't play. I was beginning to think something else was going on though. Last week, JC pointed out that some of Slick's men were following me. I made a mental note to ask Michael about Pork if I could ever catch him by himself.

Michael and I shared a crib while my mom stayed in an apartment on the north side. To her dismay, I didn't stay with her but with my older brother. With the things I did, I thought it was best to do so. She didn't need that type of drama in her house.

I was in for the night, so I decided to take a hot shower. I let the hot water run down my back, easing the pain that lingered from earlier. Later that night, visions of Crystal filled my head as I closed my eyes and drifted off to sleep.

"Ty, wake up," I heard Michael say.

I slowly opened my eyes. It took me a minute to adjust to the darkness. "Man, what time is it?"

Michael stood there with an overstuffed duffle bag right next to him. "I'm going to have to lay low for a few days. That is, until things cool down."

By now I'm fully awake. Curious to know what was going on. "What's up?"

"These dudes I've been working with turned on me, man. They tried to set me up with the Feds. Slick wants me to get out of town for a few days. I'll be in Vegas." Michael threw a phone on the bed. I picked it up.

"My number is on there. I had to dump my other one."

"But what about me? I need time to pack."

"Lil bro, you're not going anywhere. I want you to continue to go to school like nothing is happening. But don't sell to anyone until we get more of a handle on this situation."

"I promised some dudes I would have something for them. They expecting it."

"Give it to them this time, but after that, I need you to lay low too. Just go to school and come straight home. Don't be roaming all over Dallas."

"Maybe I should just go with you."

"Naw. I need to be alone for a minute, so I can think about my next move. Slick will have someone watch the crib, so you should be safe."

I didn't feel safe if Slick's men were watching me. In fact, that smelled like danger to me. "I don't need them watching me. I can watch out for myself," I responded.

"It's some more stuff going on that I can't talk about right now. Don't argue with me on this."

"Whatever, man. Do you and I'm going to be here doing me, believe that."

Michael stood. "I love you, man."

"Love you too, big bro."

He headed toward the door. "I'll call you on that phone when I get to Vegas."

Without another word, my brother was gone and sleep was no longer on my mind.

CHAPTER FIVE
CRYSTAL

"Crystal, wake up. It's time for school," Hope said.

With all that had happened with Sade, I hadn't kept up with my studies. Mondays were hard enough, so I dreaded going back to school.

I slowly dressed. My bus was pulling off right when I walked around the corner. Cursing under my breath, I dropped my head and walked slowly toward the house. Mom was going to be pissed, but it couldn't be avoided.

A horn blew. I looked up and saw a silver Dodge Charger. The window rolled down. "Need a ride?" Ty's husky voice asked.

I kept walking. The car crept beside me. Ty yelled, "I won't bite. I can drop you off at school since it seems like you missed your bus."

I stopped. I had two choices. Either listen to my mom lecture me, or get a ride and listen to some lame game this joker would sure try to spit. I shifted my backpack on my shoulder and walked to Ty's car. Before getting in, I said,

"I'm only doing this because I really don't want to be late today."

He laughed. "Come on. I'll make sure I get you there on time."

I threw the backpack on the backseat and hopped in the front. I eased the seatbelt over my shoulder and clamped it in.

"Thank you. I really appreciate you giving me a ride. I go to Booker T. Washington High School for Performing and Visual Arts," I said.

"I know," he responded.

He wouldn't stop smiling and showing off those perfect white teeth. His radiant smile seemed to bring a sunshine of its own. His smile was contagious. I couldn't help but smile in return.

"So what you doing over here?" I asked.

"I stopped by to pick up JC, but he wasn't feeling well," Ty said.

"How long you been knowing JC?" I asked.

"Since grade school," he responded.

"You stay over this way?"

"Used to, but now I stay in Pleasant Grove."

"Oh, okay. I got cousins that live over there. Well, in Mesquite, anyway."

"Yeah, that's right up the road."

I wanted to know as much as I could about Tyreek. "Ty, it is okay if I call you that?"

"Of course. That means you feel comfortable enough around me to do so. Only my teachers call me Tyreek."

"Well, Ty, how old are you?"

"I'll be seventeen next month," he responded.

"Really, I'll be sixteen next month. What day?" I asked.

"On the sixteenth."

"Wow! Mine is on the sixteenth too."

"Cool. Then we need to do something special since we're birthday twins."

"Well, I don't know you like that, but okay."

"You allowing me to take you to school is a start. By next month, I plan to get to know you very well, Crystal. That is, if you'll let me."

"I'll think about it," I said with a huge smile on my face.

One of Chris Brown's latest songs came on the radio. I bobbed my head. "Ooh, that's my song there," I said.

Ty turned up the volume. We drove the rest of the way to school in silence while enjoying the music.

Ty pulled up in the first vacant parking spot. To my surprise, he got out. "What are you doing?" I asked.

"Walking you to the front door," he responded and passed me my backpack.

"You don't have to do that."

"But I want to." He flashed his pearly white teeth.

Some of the girls stared our way as we walked up the walkway to the front of the school. We went through the normal drill of going through the metal detectors. "I can drop you back at home afterward if you like," Ty said once we stood in the hall.

I thought about it. "I can catch the bus."

"You sure?" he asked, looking a little disappointed.

"I'm sure." Without saying another word, I left Ty standing there and went to my homeroom class.

I could barely concentrate on anything because I couldn't get Ty off my mind. I loved everything about him. Like his smooth brown skin and how he looked at me with a twinkle in his dark brown eyes. His smile was contagious. Made me feel all giddy inside. His deep voice sent chills through my body. Ty was no Chris Brown, but he definitely had my attention.

At 2:15 p.m., I rushed out the front door of the school to catch my bus. There was Ty leaning on his car with his arms crossed waiting on me. I pretended like I didn't see him.

"Your limo awaits," Ty said as he opened the passenger door.

I stopped and looked at him. "I thought I told you I was riding the bus." I ignored the stares from others.

"I know, but why ride the bus when you have me?"

Good point. "I need for you to take me straight home."

He smiled as he moved out of the way so I could get in the car. "I'll be on my best behavior. Promise." Ty eased through the line of cars until we were driving down the road headed to my neighborhood.

This time we rode with the windows down, and the nice spring breeze felt good as I tried to figure out who Ty was.

"You want a burger or something?" he asked.

"I'm straight." My growling stomach, however, gave me away. I really was hungry. The food in the cafeteria wasn't too appetizing, so I only ate an apple and drank some juice for lunch. I was practically starving.

"I think your stomach disagrees. Mickey D's right there."

"I don't have any money," I responded.

"Didn't ask you that."

Without hesitating, Ty pulled up in the parking lot and then exited the car. Ten minutes later, he came back with burger, fries, and drinks for the both of us.

"Thank you, but you didn't have to," I said.

"I know. I wanted to." He winked and handed me my food. "You know you're special, because I normally don't like anybody eating in my car."

"Oh. Well, excuse me. I'll wait until I get home," I said.

"No. I just wanted to take the time to let you know that you are special."

I blushed. "You know it. And don't you ever forget it either." I ate my food while Ty drove me home. During the ride, I caught him glancing at me, but I didn't care. I was hungry.

He pulled up in front of my house. "Thanks for the ride."

"Anytime."

Ty got out and opened my door. He was such a gentleman. He walked with me up the walkway. I stopped halfway to the front porch. "My dad's inside, so this is probably as far as you should go."

Ty shrugged. "I understand. So can I call you later?"

"I got a lot of homework so I'll call you."

"Promise?" he asked as he put his hands in his pocket.

"I never make a promise that I don't keep."

"Crystal!" my father yelled from the front door.

"I better go," I whispered, rushing to the porch, hoping Ty was quickly on his way back to his car.

"Who's that?" my dad asked.

"One of JC's friends," I responded as I eased past him and went into the house.

"Then what is he doing over here?"

I stopped walking and came face to face with my dad. "He was telling me JC's not feeling well. I'm going to go check on him later."

"Be sure that's all it is. You are too young to be dating."

"My mind is on my books."

"Be sure you keep it on your books." I could smell the alcohol on my dad's breath.

"Yes, Daddy," I responded, doing my best to avoid any type of confrontation.

I did my usual after school ritual minus fixing me a sandwich. I grabbed my cell phone and headed across the street to check on JC.

CHAPTER SIX
TY

After dropping Crystal off, I headed to a few of my brother's hang out spots to see if I could catch up with some of his boys. I'd tried to reach Michael all day, but he wasn't returning my calls nor my texts. It had been less than twenty-four hours, but we always stayed in contact.

"He's out of town is all I know," one of my brother's best friends named Jay said.

"If he calls you, let me know."

I wasn't ready to go home, so I drove through South Dallas before heading back to Pleasant Grove. As I passed by their street, I thought I caught a glimpse of Crystal. I was tempted to call her, but I would be patient and wait for her call. After rambling through my CD case, I slipped in one of my brother's favorite rappers, Tupac, who soon became my favorite, and then drove to the crib.

The hairs on the back of my neck stood up the closer I got to the front door. I inserted the key into the lock, but the door fell open without me turning the key.

"What in the world?" I said out loud. The entire house looked like a tornado had been through it. I pulled out my gun as I went room by room to see if anyone was still there. Nothing. *Where were Slick's men? The men who were supposed to watch the place? If they were outside, then how did someone get in and do this to us?* I retrieved the phone Michael gave me out of my pocket and sent a text message with 911 on the end. A few minutes later, the phone rang.

"Lil bro, what's up?" Michael asked.

Trying not to sound hysterical, I said, "Somebody broke in. Stuff is everywhere. I don't know if they was looking for something or somebody. They tried to make it look like a robbery but ain't nothing missing."

"Calm down," he said.

"Calm down. Nigga, you calm down. You get ghost like five-o after you, and now somebody's violated our house. I need you here. When you coming back from Vegas?"

"I'm going to catch the first flight back. I see me leaving is not going to solve anything."

"Man, what's going on? You still got me in the dark."

"Ty, pack up a bag or two. Get some money out the safe and then go to a secure location. I'll be in touch."

"But . . ." Michael hung up before I could ask him any more questions.

I wasn't going to front. I was scared. Yeah, I talked a good game, but for the most part, I never had to deal with this type of drama. Normally, my brother kept everything under control. I needed to find a hideout spot. I couldn't go to my mom's because I didn't want to bring any type of drama to her front porch. Besides, my brother sort of lied and told everybody that our mama was dead. I guess so no one would think they could get to her to get to him in a dire situation.

Although I missed my mama and wanted to run home to her, I knew I couldn't. Think. I had to think. Where could I go? My phone rang. JC's name displayed on the screen. "Man, I can't talk right now. I got a dilemma."

"What's up?"

"My brother got himself mixed up in something, and I need to lay low."

"Come crash over here. I got bunk beds. You know my mama don't care. She'll be glad to have you over here."

"I don't know, man. I don't want to put y'all in harm's way."

"You know I'm packing heat. Ain't nobody coming over here. I'm GD's son. GD might be locked up, but his name still make niggas sweat."

True. JC's dad was an OG. One of the original old gangstas. He would kill a man if he looked at him wrong. JC had respect on the streets because the apple didn't fall that far from the tree. I'd never known JC to kill anyone, but he did have a mean streak. A side I rarely saw, but when I did, I moved the hell out of his way.

"I'll be there as soon as I pack up me some stuff," I said as I found a huge duffle bag and threw some clothes in there. I only planned on being gone a few days.

"Bring that PlayStation game," JC said.

"I got you." I hung up the phone with JC, and then I finished packing.

I was halfway out the door when I remembered the game, so I turned and picked it up off the floor and grabbed a few other games to keep my mind off things. I looked back at the living room one last time before leaving to go to JC's.

CHAPTER SEVEN
CRYSTAL

Dear Diary,

I should be studying but I can't stop thinking about Ty. He is so cute. He's the perfect height. He has the perfect smile. His eyes twinkle when he laughs. I just love everything about him. I get so nervous when I'm around him.

There go my parents arguing again. They should be tired because they are wearing me out.

Well, Diary, I'll end my note here. Will check in with you later.

"Kevin, I work all day. The least you could do is clean up around here!" my mom yelled.

I heard something slam against the wall and assumed my dad threw something. Dang, I wasn't in the mood for another round of Jackson mania. So I grabbed by iPod and slipped out the front door and sat on the porch. I tuned in to one of Nicki Minaj's latest tracks and rapped along with the lyrics. Listening to music always eased my mind. I closed my eyes and pretended to be somewhere other than here.

"I guess since you're not going to call me, I'm going to have to call you," Ty said.

I jolted straight up and opened my eyes. "What are you doing here?" I stuttered.

Ty leaned forward. I got a whiff of his woodsy cologne. "Was at JC's. Saw you sitting on the porch. Thought I would come over."

I pulled the headphones from my ears and gave Ty my full attention. "I was going to call. Just got a lot going on."

"What's up? Talk to me." Ty took the liberty of taking a seat next to me.

"Just dealing with some family issues right now," I responded.

"Tell me your secrets, and I'll tell you mine," he said as he looked at me.

I broke the stare and looked toward the bottom step. My parents had moved their argument to the living room. We could hear them yelling all the way from the porch. I stood up. "Walk with me."

Ty obeyed and walked beside me as we walked out the yard and down the sidewalk through the neighborhood.

"My parents are always arguing, and it's really getting on my nerves."

He kicked a can to the side of the curb. "You're lucky to have two parents. I don't know where my dad is."

I rolled my eyes. "I guess. Sometimes I wish my dad would leave. At least him and my mom wouldn't be around each other, and we would have peace in our house."

Ty reached for my hand. I didn't pull back. We continued to walk and talk. "It's not that bad, is it?"

I stopped walking. "Trust me when I say it's like World War III up in that house almost every single day. The only peace I get is when I go to school, or when I'm sitting out on the porch."

"Sorry that you have to deal with that. Grown ups got a lot of issues, so try not to let it get to you."

"I hate to say this, but sometimes I wish they would divorce. I think it would be best for everybody."

Ty squeezed my hand and looked down into my eyes. "You don't mean that. Maybe they'll work it out."

I got lost in his eyes, briefly forgetting we were talking about my parents. My mind wandered to places it had never wandered to before. I could hear my heartbeat go pitter-patter. A silly smile filled my face. I looked away in embarrassment, jerked my hand away, and turned to walk back toward my house. "I better get back home before they realize I'm gone," I said.

Ty picked up his pace to keep up with me. "Crystal, wait." The plea in his voice caused me to stop. He reached for my hand, and I let him hold it.

"What Ty?"

"I know we just met, but if I don't say this now, I might lose my nerves."

I tapped my foot. "I'm waiting."

"You're going through your thing with your parents, and I'm sort of going through something with my brother. Maybe we can be there for each other and help each other with our problem."

"And how do you think we're supposed to do that?" I asked.

"Promise to listen. Sometimes just talking about it helps."

I could do that. Ty was a good listener, and he seemed to offer some good advice. Now I was a little curious to know what kind of problems he was having with his brother. "So what's up with your brother?" I asked.

"Tonight's about you. We'll talk about him another time."

"You sure? You seem to have a lot on your mind too."

"It can wait until another time. Right now, I just want to make sure you're okay with everything."

"I'm as okay as I can be under the circumstance," I responded.

My cell phone rang. I pulled it out of my pocket because it was the ring tone I had set for Sade. "This my bestie." I removed my hand from his embrace. Sade sounded upset on the other end. "Give me a few minutes and I'll call you right back," I told her. Then I looked at Ty. By now we're standing in front of my house. "I will call you later. I promise." Without another word, I walked to the house.

CHAPTER EIGHT
TY

I watched Crystal go back into her house. She promised to call, but she had said those same words the last time, so I wasn't too confident that she would. I wanted to follow her, but she'd dialed her friend back. Besides, I did have a little pride about myself. I don't sweat girls, they sweat me. I had an image to uphold. Who was I fooling? I would sweat Crystal until she came around. There's nothing I wouldn't do to get to know her.

JC was playing a video game when I went back in the house. His mom was still gone, so we had the house to ourselves.

"I see you making leeway with my girl across the street."

"I wouldn't say all of that," I responded as I opened up a soda and sat on the couch next to him.

"Man, don't hurt her or I'll have to put a hurting on you," JC teased.

"Oh, we good. Crystal might not know it, but she got my heart already."

JC put the remote down. "Aw man, don't tell me it's some of that love at first sight crap. You can't go out like that, dog."

I shrugged my shoulders. "It is what it is. There's something about Crystal, and I'm determined to play this out."

JC picked up the remote. "I never would have imagined you falling in love. You ain't even hit it yet."

"Sex ain't everything." I took a drink of my soda.

"As long as I put a glove on it, that's all I want from a shorty is that sweet stuff between her legs."

"Man, find you one shorty and you might can get some love without a glove."

JC nodded. "You're right. When I find one worthy to be with the prince of Dallas, then I will."

We sat in the living room and played an NBA game on the PlayStation. The cell phone ringing made me lose my concentration. I missed the last shot. "You lucky my phone rang." I picked up the phone and smiled when I saw it was Crystal.

"Luck ain't got nothing to do with it. Skills, man, I got skills." JC stuck out his chest.

"Surprised you called," I said to Crystal when I answered.

"I told you I would," she responded.

"But still. You ran to your front door so fast, I thought I had said or did something." I'd gotten off the couch and went to sit on the front porch. It was dark outside, so if anyone looked in my direction, they wouldn't be able to see me.

"My best friend needed me. She's been dealing with a lot lately."

My phone beeped. I didn't recognize the number, so I let the call go to voice mail and continued talking to Crystal. "You're a good friend. You seem to be there for everybody else. Let me be there for you." Something about Crystal made me want to be her protector.

"I'm okay. What's going on with you and your brother?" she asked.

I sort of regretted telling her that I had issues with my brother. We were just getting to know each other, so I didn't want her to know I was involved in the drug game. "Just family things."

"That's not fair. I opened up to you about my parents, but you're trying to be all secretive."

I leaned back on the porch. "My brother works for Slick. I know you've heard of him."

"Who hasn't? He's definitely known around these parts," Crystal responded.

"Well, my brother is high up in his organization. He only started doing it to help take care of my mama and me."

"He did what he had to do, I guess."

I nodded, glad that Crystal understood. *But how would she feel if she found out what I did?* For now, I would keep it a secret. "Lately, some strange things have been going on."

"I'm all ears," Crystal responded.

"I think my brother has done something against Slick, and now they are looking to kill him or something."

"Oh my goodness, Tyreek. Do you think you're safe? Is your brother alright?" Crystal blurted out question after question.

"I don't know. The reason I'm at JC's is because he told me to lay low." I told Crystal about some of the events that led me to this point.

"I don't know what to say. I just met you. I don't want to lose you already."

Her concern really touched my heart. "I'm fine. It's my brother whose life is in jeopardy. If they were going to do something to me, they would have already. Don't you think?"

"Ty, I hope you're right."

I was beginning to think I shouldn't have told Crystal anything. I didn't want to scare her away. "Thanks for listening. I'm a little scared, but it's not like I can tell JC that. He's my boy and things, but I don't want him to think I'm soft or anything."

"Your secret is safe with me," Crystal responded.

Little did she know I had another secret. A secret I hoped she'd never find out.

CHAPTER NINE
CRYSTAL

Dear Diary,
It's hard to sleep after the bombshell Ty dropped on me. I need to get a handle on my emotions. My mom and dad warned me about messing with neighborhood hustlers, but Ty's not like that. Yes, his brother is deep in the game, but Ty is different. He goes to school. He treats me with respect. He's smart. He's nothing like some of the guys I go to school with.

I closed my diary and dialed Dena's phone number. "Dena, what are you doing?" I asked, because I needed to talk to someone.

"Chillin'. What's up with you?" she responded from the other end of the phone.

"I met this cute guy. He's one of JC's friends, and I think I'm in love," I blurted out.

"Hold the press. When did this happen? And why are you just now telling me?"

"I've seen him over at JC's, but I officially met him the day of the funeral."

"That's only been a week, so why are you already talking about love?"

"It's just something about him. I can't put my finger on it. I just know that I love him."

"You just started talking to him, so it can't be love," Dena responded.

"You're really trying to mess up this natural high I'm on." I lay back on my bed.

"So who is he? Details. I need details."

"His name is Tyreek. He's about six feet tall. Not too big and not too small. Just right. He has dark brown eyes that are to die for. Oh my goodness! He's everything I've ever wanted."

"Did you say Tyreek?"

"Yes, you know him?" I sat up in bed.

"On the streets he's known as Doughboy."

"Everybody got a nickname, so what?"

"Doughboy. Get it? He has plenty of money also known as dough because of the type of work he does."

"I'm not following you," I responded.

"How you think some of the kids at school are getting their drug habits satisfied? Somebody has to be supplying them, right?"

A light bulb went off in my head. "I should have known. He told me his brother is one of Slick's top dogs."

"Then you know he's in the drug game too, so why you tripping about it now?" Dena asked.

"I'm not tripping. I just don't like him lying to me."

"I probably would have lied to you too. Sometimes you can act a little green," Dena said.

I pouted. "I'm no square."

Dena laughed. "You're right. You are as straight as they come. If you like Tyreek, so what. Him selling dope ain't got to interfere with y'all relationship."

"You know my mama and daddy ain't going for that. My dad don't want me dating, period."

"You'll be sixteen in another month. Come on now. Your dad needs to give you a break."

Whether he was drunk or not, my dad was very serious when it came to me and dating boys. If it was up to him, I would be a thirty-year-old virgin. I chatted with Dena for the next thirty minutes. As soon as I hung up with her, I dialed Ty's number. The call went to voice mail, and I decided not to leave a message.

I drifted off to sleep dreaming about Ty. I woke up feeling a little pain on my side, so I rolled over only to discover that I had slept on my phone. Ty's number displayed as a missed call. I had to get ready for school, so I pushed Ty to the back of my mind and went into the kitchen.

"How's my favorite girl doing?" my dad said from behind the newspaper as he sat at the table.

"I thought I was your favorite," my little sister responded.

"You're both my favorite." He winked.

I loved it when my dad was in a jovial mood. It reminded me of better times. It reminded me of two years ago before he lost his job at the phone company. Those were much happier times.

"Kevin, can you at least take Hope to school? She has this science project. So she won't be able to ride the bus, and I got an important meeting," Mom said as she poured herself some juice.

"I wish you would have said something to me last night," he responded.

Mom slammed the glass on the counter, almost breaking it. "Either you can or you can't."

"I guess."

"Fine! Hope, go put your stuff in your dad's truck. I'll see you both when I get home this evening," Mom said as she looked in my direction.

I remained silent. The tension in the air between my parents frightened me. He sat in his chair glaring at her, and she stood by the counter glaring at him. Neither wanted to be the first to back down, I guess.

The sound of the microwave must have startled my mom because she looked at it. "Oh my goodness. I'm going to be late. Bye y'all," she said, leaving the kitchen without looking back.

"I don't know what to say about your mama. Those people at her job treat her like a slave, and then she wants to come home and take it out on me. I'm not having it. I tell you, I'm not having it," Dad said.

Hope returned to the kitchen. "I'm ready, Dad." He mumbled some things I couldn't understand as he left the room behind Hope.

I poured myself a bowl of cereal and ate it as fast as I could. I rushed out the front door and ran to catch the bus that was pulling off just as soon as I made it to the corner. Almost out of breath, I threw my hands in the air. Now I had to scramble to find some change to catch the city bus. A horn blew. I looked up and smiled when I saw the window of Ty's car roll down.

"Your prince charming to the rescue, again," Ty said.

"Glad you're still here, because I have a bone to pick with you," I said as I opened the door and threw my backpack on the backseat. Ty had a "what did I do" look on his face. I didn't like being lied to, and Ty was about to find that out.

CHAPTER TEN
TY

"When were you going to tell me about your side hustle?" Crystal blurted out as soon as she got in the car.

"I was going to tell you when the time was right," I responded.

"The perfect time to bring it up would have been when we were talking about your brother, but no, I had to hear it from someone else," she snapped.

I drove and listened to Crystal go on and on about me not telling her about selling drugs. It's nothing I'm proud of. What did she expect? Hey, my name is Tyreek, and I'm a drug dealer. I knew she would find out. But I should have been the one to tell her. Why didn't I tell her when I was telling her about Michael? Because I did care what she thought of me.

I stopped at the light. "Crystal, I'm sorry for not telling you I sell, okay? I'm not proud of that. I only sell to students who ask. It's not like I'm on the corner slanging."

"And that makes it right? Ty, you're in school. You have the opportunity to do something different with your life." Crystal really sounded like she believed in me. She'd just met me, yet she believed that I could be better than just a neighborhood drug dealer.

"My brother does the heavy stuff. I just go around to the schools."

"But, Ty. You and I both know that's not cool. What if you get caught? I know you don't want to go to jail. You're too smart for that." I tried not to think about negative possibilities. Crystal was throwing it all out there.

"I got to do what I got to do." I looked away.

"I don't like it." Crystal folded her arms, leaned closer to the door, and looked out the window.

"But do you like me?" I hoped her attitude toward what I did wouldn't change how she felt about me.

"A little," she confessed as she now turned and faced me.

"You sure it's not a lot?" I responded, feeling like I had a little hope.

Crystal's eyes lit up when she smiled. "Okay, I like you a whole lot. Just don't come around me with the stuff."

"Fine, I won't," I lied. I couldn't really promise her that, especially since I had some bags of pills hidden in my backpack. I reached over to touch her hand, when my body jerked from the bump to my car's rear end.

"What the hell!" I yelled out, and then looked at Crystal. "Are you okay?"

"I'm not sure. What just happened?" Crystal looked back to see what hit us.

I looked in my rearview mirror. A gray Lincoln pulled up on the side of me. My hand automatically went to the weapon under my leg. I grasped it just in case.

"Tell Big Mike we want our money," a man I didn't recognize yelled from the Lincoln.

"Who the hell are you?" I yelled, trying to act all hard, but I was really scared inside.

"He knows who I am." The passenger mean mugged me before rolling the window up. With no regard for my life, the Lincoln cut in front of me and then sped off.

Crystal looked at me with huge doe eyes and her mouth half open. "Oh my God! What's going on, Ty?"

"Baby girl, I don't know. I'm going to get you to school and try to track down my brother," I responded.

We were only blocks away from her school. "I can go with you if you want."

Shocked, I responded, "Are you serious?"

"Ty, you shouldn't have to go through this alone."

Crystal was my ride or die chick for sure. "Crystal, look. I appreciate it, but I think this is something I need to do myself." She pouted, but I didn't care. I dropped her off in front of the school.

"Text me to let me know you're okay," Crystal said, right before exiting the car.

"I will. I'll see you later. Promise you that."

I pulled out the phone Michael had given me and dialed his number. No answer. I dialed his number again and this time he answered.

"Man, where are you? I thought you were coming back to Dallas," I yelled.

"I'm here. Shouldn't you be in school?"

"I would be if somebody who you know didn't try to rear-end me this morning." I told Michael what happened.

He yelled, "Meet me at Jay's ASAP."

I did an illegal U-turn, hoping there weren't any cops around and hopped on the freeway. The bumper-to-bumper traffic did nothing to calm my nerves. I knew I shouldn't be texting and driving, but I sent Crystal a quick text to let her know I located my brother. She sent me a smiley face in return.

For it to be morning, a lot of people were out on Jay's block. I found the first available parking spot and rushed to the front door. One of Jay's boys recognized me.

"Go on in, Doughboy. They in the back."

"All right, man," I said, looking around as I walked through the back. This wasn't my first time at Jay's place, so I knew exactly where they were. In the den. Jay, my brother, and some other dude that I didn't know were seated. When they noticed me enter, they got quiet.

"Nick, this my lil bro, Doughboy."

He extended his hand. "Hey, heard a lot about you."

"What's up?" I responded with a head nod.

"Have a seat. Want something to drink?" Jay asked.

Michael responded for me. "Naw. He's all right."

Ironically, Michael didn't want me drinking or smoking. If I did sneak a drink, I made sure never to do it around him. I saw what drugs did to people, so he didn't ever have to worry about me slipping up and sampling the merchandise.

Jay and the dude named Nick left Michael and me alone. Michael stood up and paced the floor. "Ty, where you laying your head?" he asked.

"At my boy's place." There was no need for me to say JC. He knew JC was the only friend that I would hang out with on that level.

"I got myself into something I might not be able to get out of." He turned and faced me. The look in his eyes caused me to shiver. I'd never seen fear in his eyes before.

"Michael, what's going on? People smashing up our place. Trying to rear-end me. Come on, man. You got to tell me something," I blurted.

"This is my battle, and I'm going to fight it. I want you to stay out of it."

"People keep putting me in it, so at least let me know what's going on so I'll know what I'm up against."

"Follow me," Michael said.

I walked out the back door with him. He looked around, and once he was sure we were all alone, he leaned close to me and said, "I copped a deal with the Feds."

"You did what!" I said louder than I probably should have.

Michael pulled me closer. "Man, I'm in so deep. I don't see no way out."

"Why man? Slick finds out, you're dead. What am I gonna tell Mama? You know with her heart, she's not going to be able to take it if something happens to you."

"I know. That's why I want you to stay where you are. First thing though, you need to get rid of that car. You got that safe deposit key I gave you, right?"

"Yes. Right here." I pulled the chain out from under my shirt that held the golden key to a safe deposit box at one of the local banks.

"Everything you need to start over is in the box. I got the money out of the house safe. I got a bag I want you to take with you. Get it before you leave."

"You acting like this is the last time I'm going to see you." Tears formed in the corner of my eyes.

"We're going to see each other again. I promise you that." Michael gave me a tight hug. I felt him slip something in my pocket. He whispered in my ear. "If anything happens to me, give this to Agent Nick."

"The dude—"

"Yes. He's undercover." Michael started laughing and teasing me. "You still can't beat me on the courts."

I played along and playfully hit him. Jay and the man whom I now knew was an undercover agent came out on the back.

Michael said, "I'm going to walk Ty out. I'll be back." He walked me outside and handed me a set of keys. "Where are your other keys?" I handed him the keys to my Charger and followed him to a black SUV. "This car is fully equipped just in case. Got bulletproof windows. Weapons are located in the frame of the doors."

After showing me the hidden compartments, Jay opened the driver's door. "Ty, take care of yourself."

"You too," I responded. Under normal circumstances, I would have been thrilled to get a new ride, but something about this just didn't seem right to me. I got behind the wheel, closed the door, and rolled the windows down.

Michael said, "Love you man."

"Love you too, bro."

"I'll be in touch," he said as he moved out of the way.

I started the SUV and left my brother, not knowing if it would be the last time I would see him.

CHAPTER ELEVEN
CRYSTAL

As soon as I got home from school, I threw my backpack on my bed and then jetted across the street to JC's house. I didn't see Ty's car, but thought JC would know something. I knocked on the door and looked back across the street, watching my dad watch me from the living room window.

"Come on in," JC said as he opened the front door.

"Have you heard from Ty?" I asked, as I walked inside.

"Oh, a brother don't even get a hug or something," JC responded.

I hugged JC. "I'm sorry. I was just worried about Ty after what happened this morning."

We took a seat on opposite ends of the couch. JC seemed to be in the dark about what happened, so I told him about the incident from this morning. "He said he was going to look for his brother."

"Ty's all right. If he wasn't, I would have heard something by now."

"Well, if you hear something call me," I responded.

"You know I will. You got a thing for my boy, I see." JC flashed a huge smile.

"You can say that."

"Crystal's got a crush," he teased.

"Whatever." I rolled my eyes.

"It's all good. He got a thing for you too. I told him he better treat you right, or he'll have to answer to me."

"You don't have to worry about that. I know how to handle myself," I responded.

"It's going to be some haters on the block when they hear you two are together," JC said.

"Well, we're really not together-together. We just met."

"Trust me. You might as well be together because my boy got feelings for you."

"Really? You're not just telling me this, are you?" I asked. My insides felt all mushy. To know that Ty felt the same way about me made me smile.

"Girl, you know I wouldn't lie to you."

I rolled my eyes. "JC, remember the time you lied about—"

"Well, I wouldn't lie to you about something as serious as this."

"Okay. Cool. You're the best." I stood up and hugged JC again. "Tell him to call me when you talk to him." I practically skipped back home with the new revelation of

Ty's feelings for me. I was glad to know that my feelings weren't one-sided.

Excited, I pulled my pink diary from its hiding place under my mattress. Then I fell on the bed and wrote an entry expressing my feelings for Ty and the information JC shared with me about Ty's feelings for me. I wrote:

Although Ty hasn't told me these things himself, I can tell he does like me. I can't wait to hear the love word directly from him, himself.

Hope burst into my room. "Mama said you're to cook us some chili dogs because she's working late tonight."

"Fine, but next time please knock."

"Whatever. Dad said you better not be over JC's talking to that boy too."

"Mind your business."

"I saw the boy. He is cute. Is he your boyfriend?"

"Maybe." I closed my diary.

"You might as well tell me because I'll find out about it later when I read your diary."

I threw a pillow at Hope. "You better not be reading my stuff."

Hope laughed and left the room without closing my door. I found a new hiding place for my diary just in case Hope wasn't joking. I placed it in a shoebox and then hid it in my closet.

An hour later, my dad, Hope, and I were seated at the dining room table eating chili dogs. Actually, we had a pleasant evening. Dad didn't seem to have had any alcohol. He told us jokes like old times.

"Since I cooked, Hope, you got to clean up the kitchen," I said after we ate.

"No, I don't," she responded.

My dad said, "Yes, Hope. Your sis did cook. The least you could do is clean up the kitchen."

I stuck my tongue out at her. Hope pouted and grabbed her and my dad's plate. I held up my empty plate and said, "You forgot something." She didn't want to pick up my plate. She looked at my dad, and then back at me and grabbed my plate. "Don't drop it," I said.

My cell phone rang. I answered, "Hi Sade. I was beginning to worry about you."

"I'm making it. I called to tell you that we're moving," Sade responded.

"Moving! Moving where?"

"Everything okay?" my dad asked. I forgot he was still sitting at the table.

"Yes. It's Sade. She says they're moving."

I got up from the table and went to sit outside on the porch. I listened as Sade went on and on about where they were moving. They were moving to an apartment near her mother's job. I couldn't believe my best friend was leaving me. Sure, she would still be in Dallas, but I was used to her being in the neighborhood where we were at least in walking distance.

"So what do you think?" Sade asked.

"I'm happy for you," I lied.

"No, you're not. I can tell by the sound of your voice."

"Are you going to try to get back into Booker T?" I asked.

"Next year. I'm going to sit the rest of this semester out and just make up for it in summer school."

"There's always the DART."

"Exactly. I'll get my mom to buy me a monthly pass. I still have money saved from when we won the contest. I'm still not giving up hope that Adore will be the next Destiny's Child."

"I'd sort of given up on our group with everything that has happened," I admitted.

"I know I've had a lot going on, but I'm better. I love to sing. I think it's time for me to get back to doing what I love to do."

It was good hearing the excitement in Sade's voice. I felt like I had my best friend back. "Get Dena on the three-way. Adore is back," I stated.

Dena was just as excited as I was about Sade's new attitude, so she called her cousin Jada, our unofficial manager. Jada said, "First thing we need to do is get you all together so you can rehearse. I talked to Manchu last week, and he said the CD should be dropping this summer. I need to get y'all some gigs. Before then, we need to get y'all some photo shoots." Jada went on and on.

None of us were able to get a word in with Jada on the phone. I heard a horn blow, and when I looked up this black SUV that I didn't recognize pulled up. The window rolled down. I smiled when I saw Ty. "Hey, got to go." I ended the call and walked across the street.

CHAPTER TWELVE
TY

"Like my new ride?" I asked Crystal when she walked over.

"Nice. What happened to the Charger?" she asked.

As I exited the SUV, she moved to the side. "My brother thought it would be best to switch up."

"So things are cool with your brother?"

"Let's just say he got a lot of stuff going on right now, but yes, we're cool." I leaned on the SUV. Crystal stood directly in front of me.

My hands automatically wrapped around her waist. One glimpse into her doe-like eyes and I knew I was instantly in love. I did what I had been wanting to do since the moment we were in close proximity of each other—leaned my head down and my lips connected with hers.

An electrical charge filled my body as our lips locked. I eased my tongue between her soft, juicy lips. There was no resistance as our tongues tangled. My body tensed up with excitement.

"Ooh, I'm going to tell Daddy," was heard from behind us.

Crystal pulled away. "That's my brat of a sister. I better go before she does."

I didn't want to let her go, but I didn't want her to get in any trouble on my account either. "Text me when you can meet me back outside," I said.

Without another word, Crystal was gone back up the walkway. I could hear her fussing at her sister as her sister ran in the house with Crystal on her heels.

I tried to block out how I felt after kissing Crystal while I told JC about Michael giving me the new SUV. We took it for a spin around the block.

"Man, this is nice. I like sitting up high," JC said as we drove down his street. "Pull up over there. There's a shorty I want to holla at."

I did as instructed. JC rolled down the passenger window and whistled. The girl was cute, but she was no Crystal. I played with the stereo system as I waited for JC to make his move.

Fifteen minutes later, he hopped back in the SUV. "I'm ready."

"So what's up with her?" I asked.

"Oh, she down with a brotha. She'll be sneaking over later tonight when my mom goes to sleep."

"So you've hit that before?" I asked out of curiosity.

"No, but I will be tonight."

"I guess I need to get ghost when she comes."

"I'm sure Crystal won't mind you hanging out with her for about an hour."

"Crystal can't date, man. She said she couldn't date until she was sixteen and that's not for another month."

"That's a bummer."

"But don't worry about me. I'll find something to get into. Even if I just sit out in my truck until you finish handling your business."

Three hours later, I was doing just that. Sitting out in my truck while JC and one of the neighborhood girls were busy doing their thang. I kept looking at Crystal's house and wondering what she was doing. Was she thinking about me? Every time I got ready to dial her number, I stopped myself. I didn't want to become a bug-a-boo.

I looked up when Crystal stormed out of the house looking upset. I jumped out of the car and ran across the street. "Hey, what's wrong?" I asked.

She fell into my arms. I held her. "I'm sick and tired of this. They won't stop fighting. I can't take this anymore."

I ran my hand through her hair. "Calm down, Crystal. Come with me. Let's go for a ride."

Crystal hesitated at first. We could hear her parents' voices. "Let me lock up, and I'll meet you at the car," she said.

An hour later, we were driving near White Rock Lake. I didn't stop because the last thing I wanted was for us to get stopped by police. Especially since I knew the SUV was fully loaded with weapons. We didn't talk much while riding. I let the music play and let her gather her thoughts. I reached over with my right hand and touched hers. She squeezed it. For the first time that night, I saw her smile.

"Thanks Ty for being here for me."

"I told you I got you."

"You probably think I'm a big baby running every time my parents fight. It's just nerve racking. I remember how they used to be. I just wish they'd divorce already and put me out of my misery."

"Crystal, that's a little dramatic, but okay." She moved her hand. "You want me to always be honest with you, right?"

"Yeah, I guess so."

"Well then, arguing isn't a reflection on you. They love you, I'm sure. They are just having some problems with one another. So stop thinking it's because of you."

Crystal leaned into the seat. "I just hate to see them like this."

"I know you do. Hopefully, they'll work it out. But if they don't, it doesn't mean they love you any less."

"Ty, don't ever change," Crystal said as she gently touched my face.

I kissed the inside of her hand. "I won't, if you won't."

Crystal's phone rang. She took the call and started giggling. I wondered who was making her laugh like that. She hung up the phone. "That was my friend, Dena. I'm in this girl group called Adore, and we have our first concert at the beginning of June at the Summer Jam."

"Wow! I didn't know my girl was a singer," I responded.

"Your girl?"

"Yes. My girl. Well, let me back up. Crystal, would you be my girl? I really like you, and I really don't want to share you with any other guy." I eased down on the brake to stop at a light.

"Let me think about it," she responded.

My heart dropped. She then said, "Yes, I'll be your girl."

I sighed, leaned over, and kissed her. A horn blew behind me. We both laughed as I pulled off and headed back to Crystal's and now my new neighborhood.

CHAPTER THIRTEEN
CRYSTAL

It's official. Ty and I are girlfriend and boyfriend.
This was one of the happiest moments of my life. I knew I
wasn't supposed to date until I turned sixteen, but that's
only a month away. Ty and I would just have to keep our
relationship a secret from my parents until then.

We pulled up in front of the house. The light was off in
the living room, so that meant my parents had probably
gone to bed. I wondered if my folks even realized I was
gone. No one had bothered to call me on my cell phone, so
they probably didn't.

Ty walked around and opened my door. He held my
hand as I exited the SUV. Our eyes locked in the moonlit
night. For the second time we kissed. I felt light on my toes
as Ty's tongue eased inside my mouth. A moan seeped out
of my mouth. I felt my body melting, but Ty held me up
with his strong masculine arms. I hated to pull away. I
could kiss him forever, but I knew I would be in deep
trouble if my parents found me.

"Thank you for turning my bad night into a night I'll never forget." I grabbed Ty's hand, but broke our connection.

"Crystal, you're the first girl I've ever felt this way about."

I found it hard to believe. Although I was still a virgin, I was not naive enough to think that a boy like Ty was one too, and hadn't been in other relationships. "There's something I need to tell you. I probably should have told you before I agreed to be your girlfriend." I took a few deep breaths and looked him straight in the eyes. Ty wore a concerned look on his face. The moonlight brightened up the area where we stood.

Ty held my hand. "You can tell me anything. It's not going to change how I feel about you."

"Not so sure about that. I'm a virgin," I blurted out before I lost my nerve.

Ty laughed. I jerked my hand away. "So it's funny?" I walked toward my house.

Ty ran up behind me. "Hold on, baby. I'm not laughing at you. I promise you that. You being a virgin is a good thing."

I stopped walking and looked at Ty. "Are you sure? Because if it's going to be a problem then maybe we shouldn't do this."

Ty reached for my hand. "Crystal, we won't do anything until you're ready. I can't promise you that it's going to be easy for me, but I care about you so much that I'm willing to wait as long as I need to."

My heart swelled as I listened to Ty. I found myself falling for him hard. "I can't make any promises. It could be soon, a year, or years."

Ty kissed the back of my hand. "Crystal, I'm sure it won't be years. Look at me." He held his chest out. "How can you resist all of this?"

I laughed. "It's going to be hard too, I'm sure."

We stood at the end of my porch. Ty said, "As much as I hate to end this night, you better go in before you get in trouble."

I glanced at the front door and eased my house key out of my pocket. "You're right."

Ty gave me a quick peck on the lips. I attempted to enter the house as quietly as I could and tiptoed through the hallway. The moment I got near their bedroom, I heard my mother and father snoring. I eased past their room and didn't breathe until I was securely in my own bedroom. When I flipped the light on, Hope smiled at me as she leaned on my bed. "Busted!" she said.

"Crap!" I mumbled. "I don't know what you're talking about."

"First, you sneak out of the house, and then I catch you kissing a boy. Wait until I tell mama about this." Hope teased me by waving the phone that showed Ty and I engaged in some serious lip-locking. I reached for the phone, but she was too quick and jumped to the other side of the bed.

"You better give me that so I can delete it, or I'm beating your behind."

"If you put one hand on me, I'm telling Mama for sure. Then you'll be grounded and no sweet sixteen birthday party for you." Hope seemed to be getting some enjoyment out of torturing me. I had to think of something and something fast. I needed a bargaining tool, because Hope couldn't show the picture of me kissing Ty to my folks. They would never agree to me dating him if they did.

"Hope, we're supposed to stick together. Why are you trying to blackmail me?"

"Because I can. Besides, I'm bored. I need something to keep me entertained."

I plopped on the bed. Hope was trapped on the other side of the bed, so I wasn't worried about her going anywhere.

"Look. I'm fifteen years old, and I don't have time to play these childish games of yours. So what if you caught me kissing Ty. He's my boyfriend."

"Oooh. I bet y'all doing the nasty too," Hope said.

"No, we're not. But even if I was, it's none of your business."

"I'm telling Mama."

"Go right ahead. If you want to stress her out even more, I'm not going to stop you."

Hope must have thought about it for a moment because she clicked a button on her cell phone. She held it up. "I deleted it, okay?"

I grabbed the phone from her and double-checked. Satisfied that the incriminating picture had been deleted, I moved out of the way so Hope could pass. I handed her the phone as she walked by me.

Once Hope was out of my room, I went to my secret hiding place and retrieved my diary. I wrote about becoming Ty's girlfriend and filled the pages with a bunch of hearts. I drifted off to sleep with the pen in my hand.

CHAPTER FOURTEEN
TY

"No, he's not here," I heard JC say from his side of the room as I drifted in and out of sleep the next morning.

I yawned and sat up in the bed. I waited for JC to end his call. "Who was that looking for me?" I asked as soon as JC ended his call.

"That was somebody looking for your brother. Man, I hate to tell you this, but there's a bounty on his head."

"Say what?" I knew Michael was in some deep mess, but now there was a bounty on his head. The thought of losing my brother made my head hurt.

"Word on the street is that he stole from one of Slick's suppliers. Slick's not too happy about it, because it's bad business. Now the supplier is willing to pay whoever brings him in one hundred thousand dollars."

"That's all. Niggas ain't going to kill for that small amount of money."

"Ty, are you crazy? Times are hard. I've seen niggas put out hits for one Benjamin."

Concerned about Michael, I dialed his number over and over until he finally decided to answer.

"This better be good. Waking me up at seven in the morning. You know I just went to sleep." Michael sounded like he was back to doing his normal routine, but wasn't anything normal about what had transpired in these last seventy-two hours.

"Michael, there's a bounty on your head for one hundred thousand."

"I heard."

"So when were you going to tell me?" I snapped. But I was trying my best not to wild out.

"Look. You need to stay out of it. As soon as I get things situated, I won't have to worry about this bounty."

"Be careful. I wouldn't even trust Jay at this point if I were you," I said. Jay had been his best friend since elementary, so I'm sure my opinion fell on deaf ears.

"You just worry about yourself right now. Is JC there?" Michael asked.

"Yes, he's right here," I responded.

"Let me talk to him for a minute," Michael said.

I handed JC the phone. He and Michael talked for a few minutes, and then Michael ended the call.

"Michael wanted me to promise to have your back if needed. You know that without a doubt."

"Man, this is some craziness. I don't even know if I should be staying here. What if somebody come after me trying to get to him?"

"You good. I told you, nobody's going to mess with you while you're under this roof. They don't want to feel the wrath of my dad."

I felt like I was running out of options. My brother's decision to turn to the Feds and steal from this supplier was causing me more drama than I cared to deal with. I wasn't sure if I wanted to continue to stay with JC, although he said it was cool. I wouldn't be able to forgive myself if something happened to him or his mom.

My cell phone rang. Crystal's name displayed. I was inches away from answering but decided not to. JC left to go to school, but I decided to stay behind. I knew what I had to do and that was to leave. I packed up my stuff. Crystal called again. I didn't want to talk to her because if I heard her voice, I wouldn't be able to leave her. I couldn't bring her into my world. I didn't know why I thought I could. With Michael's life in danger and possibly mine, I had to do whatever it took to protect Crystal.

My phone chirped. I read the text message from Crystal asking if I was okay, but I ignored it as well. I left a note and a few hundred dollar bills on the dresser, so JC would be able to find it when he returned.

Just as I opened the front door, I came face to face with the last person I expected to see. "Crystal, why aren't you at school?" I asked. She stood with a shocked look on her face.

"Because once again, I missed my bus. I just wanted to see if you could take me to school, but I guess I caught you at a bad time." She looked down at me carrying my huge duffle bag.

"Well, uh, yeah. I was headed out, but I can drop you off at school."

Crystal stared at me with her huge, baby doe brown eyes. "Are you leaving, Ty?"

"Sort of, but it's not what you think."

"So you were going to leave without telling me good-bye?" she asked. I could see tears forming in her eyes.

I dropped the duffle bag and reached for her hand, which she snatched back. "I was going to call you. I wasn't going to just walk out your life." I didn't sound too convincing. I think Crystal knew I was lying. My plans were to avoid her calls until she got tired of reaching out to me. If she got angry, maybe she would stop contacting me, and it would be easier for her to get over me. At least that's what I told myself.

Crystal yelled, "We've only been a couple for one day, and you're already tired of me."

"No, baby, that's not it. My brother is involved in so much stuff right now. I didn't want to bring you into my world."

"Too late. I became a part of your world the moment you kissed me." Crystal walked away. She stopped and turned. "I'll catch the city bus, so don't worry about taking me to school."

"Crystal, come on now. Please try and understand."

Crystal threw up the peace sign and said, "Deuces."

I watched her walk down the street. I should have gone after her, but I didn't. Instead, I got in my SUV and started driving in the opposite direction.

Pow! Pow! Several gunshots rang out from another part of the neighborhood. I swerved the car around and sped through the side streets. There my girl was, along with another woman lurched behind the bus stop seat. My tires screeched as I pulled up to the curb. "Crystal, get in!" I yelled and pushed the door open and she jumped in. I sped away just in case whoever was behind the gunshots returned.

CHAPTER FIFTEEN
CRYSTAL

Ty didn't know how happy I was to see him pull up. I forgot all about being mad at him and about him running away without telling me bye. His SUV represented safety, and I jumped in as soon as he pulled up.

"What happened?" Ty asked.

As soon as I was able to catch my breath, I said, "I was standing at the bus stop talking to that woman, and out of nowhere this blue car slows down and somebody leaned out the window and started shooting. By the time they got to the bus stop, we were laying low. Bullets were flying everywhere."

"I'm just glad you weren't hit," Ty said.

"You and me both."

Police sirens blasted through the streets as Ty and I left the neighborhood. He drove in the direction of my school, but I was too shaken up to go. Ty pulled his car in front of the school, but I didn't move.

"You don't have to be scared, Crystal. I think you're safe here."

My hand shook as I grabbed the latch on the door. "I've never been that close to bullets. I thought I was going to die."

"Baby, God got you. I got you. Don't worry about a thing."

"Easier said than done," I said as the SUV door opened.

"I'll be back at two fifteen to pick you up. I don't want you riding the bus home after what happened this morning."

I looked at Ty and saw the concerned look on his face. "Thanks. I feel a little more at ease now."

"If you need me, call me on my cell. I got a few things to take care of. I promise you I'm not going anywhere now," he said.

I walked to the front of the school but kept looking over my shoulder. Ty remained parked on the curb watching me. When I made it to the front door, I turned and waved. I went through the normal security check. The day at school seemed to drag by. I couldn't fully concentrate while in any of my classes. My mind kept flashing back to my experience at the bus stop.

"Ms. Crystal, I asked you a question," my history teacher said as she tapped on my desk, bringing me out of my daydream.

"Yes, Ms. Langley. Sorry. Just have a lot on my mind."

"I need to see you after class," she snapped, right before going back to her lecture.

I rolled my eyes as she turned her back to me. She had never been one of my favorite teachers. I don't know why she was complaining, because I was a good student. She needed to let up. I could afford not to pay attention one day out of an entire school year.

Sixth period ended. I stayed seated as my classmates left the room. I sat up straight in my desk. Ms. Langley leaned in front of her desk. "Crystal, what is going on with you? For the past few weeks I've noticed a change in you. You used to be one of my best students."

I shrugged. "I have a lot going on." I didn't feel like going into it with her. It wasn't her business that my best friend had lost her baby, or that this morning I was inches away from being another statistic as a murder victim.

"We do have school counselors that are here to help. I can recommend you to one."

"I'll be all right. I don't need to see a counselor."

"You're a really good student. I just hate to see you fall short of what I know is your full potential."

"I'll be back on track. Just dealing with some things right now, like I said."

"Okay, Ms. Crystal. But know that you're not alone. If you need someone to talk to that's what we're here for."

"Yes, ma'am." I grabbed my backpack and rushed out the door. The school buses were loading up. I walked to the end of the walkway in search of Ty's SUV. He was a no show. I hung my head down in disappointment and turned to go find my bus.

"Crystal!" I heard Ty yell. I smiled. Glad that he hadn't left me stranded, I turned and headed to his SUV. He held the door open. I didn't say a word as I eased past him and hopped in the passenger seat. A few seconds later, he was seated behind the steering wheel easing by the school buses.

"I thought you weren't coming for a minute," I confessed.

"I lost track of time," he responded.

I noticed we weren't going in the direction of my house. Instead, we were pulling up in front of Chase Bank.

"I hope you're not going to rob a bank because if so let me out now."

Ty looked at me and laughed. "You're serious, aren't you?"

"I'm just saying. This ain't no Bonnie and Clyde thing we got going on."

"Oh, you're not my ride or die chick?" he asked as his eyes twinkled.

"Oh, I can be that, but I will not be a part of no bank robbery."

He held up his hand. "Calm down. I'm not going to rob this bank. I have an account here, and I'm going to make a withdrawal. Is that okay with you?"

I felt so embarrassed. With egg on my face, I responded, "Sorry. I shouldn't have assumed you were going to do anything illegal."

"You're right. You shouldn't have." Ty shook his head before exiting the SUV, leaving me alone with my thoughts.

I sat in the car and watched different people go in and out of the bank. Very few looked like Ty, but still I shouldn't have pre-judged him. Society did enough of that. I hoped he would forgive me for thinking the worst.

Bored, while waiting on Ty to return, I flipped the ignition so the radio would come on. I turned to my favorite radio station K104 and listened to Drake spit lyrics from his latest CD. I jumped when I heard the tap on my window and almost peed on myself. When I saw Ty's face, I immediately felt relieved.

He got in the car. "With everything going on, I need you to start being more aware of your surroundings," he said as he turned on the ignition.

"I'm still jumpy from earlier," I said, feeling a little on the defensive.

"Have you ever shot a gun before?" he asked.

"No, because I've never had a reason to," I responded.

"What time do you need to be home?"

I glanced at the clock on the dashboard. I called my dad and lied to him about having to stay after school. I hope I wouldn't regret trusting Ty as he pulled the SUV on to the freeway.

CHAPTER SIXTEEN
TY

I tried to run away from my problems, but mostly run away from Crystal to keep her safe. But when the incident happened this morning, I realized I couldn't run. I had to stay and face whatever came my way. Just in case the drive-by shooting this morning wasn't something random. I definitely couldn't leave Crystal wide open.

Most of the day I tried to track down my brother, but he was in hiding and wasn't even responding to any of my phone calls. Then I realized that I was literally on my own. Seeing Crystal in a vulnerable state also got me to thinking. She lived and grew up in the hood, but she wasn't a hood girl. She had no clue how to protect herself. I couldn't have her out there defenseless.

I drove to a remote place outside of Dallas city limits. I pulled up to the gate and rolled down my window. The big armed guard said, "What's up, Doughboy?"

"Nothing much. Just wanted to bring my girl out here to the shooting range."

"It's all good. You straight," he responded.

"What is this?" Crystal asked.

"This is where some of the guys come to train that work with my brother."

"Oh." Crystal's face cringed.

"Everybody here is cool. Don't look like too many people are here, so we practically have the place to ourselves."

I could sense Crystal was a little uncomfortable and tried to ease the tension as we walked through the security point. The first order of business was getting her a weapon she would be comfortable with.

"Billy, I need something light weight but with a lot of punch," I stated as we walked up to the counter that held all sorts of weapons.

Billy was an older guy who had been a part of Slick's organization probably from the beginning. "I know exactly what this little lady needs," he replied.

Crystal said, "Ty, I'm not so sure about this."

"You trust me, right?"

Crystal looked up at me. ". . . Yes."

"If I didn't think you needed to learn, I wouldn't have brought you here. I want you to be able to take care of yourself."

"But . . ."

Before she could protest any further, Billy returned with a small semi-automatic weapon with a pink tip. The gun was small enough to fit in the palm of my hand, yet powerful enough to pack a good punch. At six rounds, this was the perfect gun for Crystal. I took the gun from Billy, and with Crystal behind me, we headed to the shooting range. To protect her ears, I placed the headphones on Crystal and then placed the gun in her hands. "Aim and shoot. Let me see how you do before I help you."

Crystal turned toward the target and pulled the trigger. She jerked back a little. "How did I do?" she asked.

Crystal's aim wasn't on target.

"With a little practice, you'll get the hang of things."

I got behind Crystal and held her arms in position. Her hair smelled good. I had to concentrate and ignore the physical reactions from being so close to her. She pulled the trigger. This time the bullet hit the target. I stayed behind her, helping her position her arms until she seemed to have the confidence to do it herself. She shot several rounds, and although not a bull's eye, she shot well enough to do bodily harm and possibly death to anyone who tried to mess with her.

"Always make sure you undo the safety clip when you get ready to aim and shoot, or your opponent will get you before you can get them." I showed Crystal how to unload the empty clip and load in the new clip.

Crystal was at first, reluctant, but now she seemed more at ease with my decision on bringing her out to the firing range. When we finished, I pulled the image of the target toward us so she could see the results of her training. "Wow, I did better than I thought I would," she said.

I turned on the safety and handed her the gun. "This is yours. I'm going to pay for it on my way out, plus load up on some ammo, and then we can hit the road back to south Dallas."

Crystal stood to the side as I took care of my business. I left the compound fully equipped.

"Are you hungry?" I asked as we reached Dallas city limits.

"Yes. I hope you didn't hear my stomach growling."

"No, I didn't hear anything," I lied.

I exited on Northwest Highway and pulled up in the Applebee's parking lot. We went inside and were seated quickly. "So many choices. I don't know what I want to eat," Crystal said, while looking over the menu.

"I'm getting some baby back ribs," I said.

"I think I'll have the same thing," Crystal responded.

Sitting there eating and talking to Crystal made me feel like things were normal. That my brother wasn't playing a dangerous game with Slick or the Feds. That my life wasn't spinning out of control because I didn't know if I had a place to lay my head. I couldn't keep staying with JC. Eventually, I would have to move and find another spot. In the meantime, I was going to continue to enjoy this meal with my girl and pretend like life was good.

CHAPTER SEVENTEEN
CRYSTAL

It was almost seven o'clock by the time I made it home. My mom's car wasn't there, so that meant she was working overtime. I hoped the gun I had hidden in my backpack didn't slip out as I tried to sneak to my room.

"I know you weren't at school this late," my dad said from behind me.

Busted. I turned and tried to wipe the guilty look from my face. "Dad, I'm trying to get this part in the school play. Things ran a little long."

"Then why is that boy dropping you off?" he snapped.

I could have played dumb and acted like I didn't know who he was referring to, but I didn't. Ty and I were a couple, so it was about time my dad got used to the idea. I was only a few weeks away from turning sixteen, so it was time for my dad to slack up a little and respect my choice. "Dad, as much as you don't want to come to terms with me growing up, I'm not a little girl anymore."

"You'll always be my little girl. Now, answer my question."

"Ty is my boyfriend, and he picked me up from school." There, I said it. Boldly, with confidence.

"So now you're dating neighborhood thugs. I thought I raised you better than that."

"Ty's not a thug. He has dreams just like I do. We both plan on doing something with our lives."

"How old is he?" Dad asked with a scorned look on his face.

"He's sixteen. His birthday is the same day as mine."

"Well, I need to meet this young man. I don't want you hanging out with no thug. You hear me?"

"Yes, sir. Ty is different."

I rushed to my room and dialed Ty's number. He answered on the first ring. "Baby, my dad wants to meet you."

"Say what?" Ty asked.

"I told my dad about us, and he wants to meet you."

"Now is not a good time. Baby, you know I got a lot going on."

"I know, but that's the only way he's going to let me keep seeing you."

Ty hesitated but responded, "I'll be over in five."

I rushed to the bathroom and freshened up. The doorbell rang. I knew it was Ty. I tried to get the door, but my dad beat me to it.

"Come in," Dad said.

Ty walked in exuding confidence. I hoped my dad didn't take it for cockiness. "Hi, Mr. Jackson. I'm Tyreek Davis."

"Hi, Ty," I said from behind my father.

"Follow me," Dad said. We both followed him into the living room. My dad pointed at the sofa. "Have a seat, son."

"Thank you," Ty responded.

"So Tyreek, what are your intentions with my daughter?"

Ty looked at me before responding to my dad. "I promise to love and protect her with my life if necessary. I will treat her with the respect she deserves."

"I want you to know she's still a virgin, and I expect her to stay that way."

My mouth flew open. I couldn't believe my dad said that. I was so embarrassed. My sex life shouldn't even be a topic of discussion. I wanted to crawl behind the sofa and hide.

Ty responded, "I respect that, and she will not be pressured by me to do anything she doesn't want to do. I love her just that much."

My dad extended his hand. "As long as we understand that, then I might give this relationship my approval."

While they were talking, the front door opened. The one thing I dreaded happened. My mom walked in before Ty could leave.

"Now, who do we have here?" Mom frowned.

"Mom, this is Ty. Ty, this is my mom."

Ty stood up and extended his hand. "I'm Tyreek Davis, and it's nice to meet you, Mrs. Jackson. I see where Crystal gets her beauty from."

Surprisingly, my mom blushed. Was this my mom? This must be the twilight zone or something.

"I see my husband is handling things up in here. Crystal, meet me in my room. Now." I almost tumbled when I jumped off the couch and followed behind her. "Shut the door," she said. I did as I was told.

"Are you still a virgin, and I want to know the truth?"

What is this concern about my sex life? "Yes, ma'am."

"I see how Tymeek looks at you."

"It's Tyreek," I corrected her.

"Tyreek or whatever his name is. I see how he looks at you. If you are having sex then maybe it's time I take you to my doctor, so we can get you on some birth control. I'm too young to be anybody's grandmother."

"But Mama, we're not doing anything."

"You young girls will lie and lie with a straight face. I'm going to make an appointment as soon as possible. I knew this day was going to come. I'm just not prepared for it." I listened as she went on and on about what she considered the birds and the bees, but little did she know I knew all about the male and female organs. I didn't need a crash course from my own mama. But I was happy that she wasn't trying to kick Ty out of my life. I stood and listened to her and pretended to soak in everything she said.

"On second thought, I'm going to take you to the clinic. Put some of my tax dollars at work. The clinic is open on Saturday, so get ready Miss Lady. We're going to get you on some birth control."

My mom had spoken, so no need in me protesting. I wasn't ready to get physical with Ty, but it wouldn't do any harm being on birth control just in case things did progress that far. I was about to turn sixteen, and after watching everything happen to Sade and other teen moms, I didn't want to be a teen mom. I had a full life ahead of me, and having a baby in tow wasn't part of my plans. I wanted to be in my twenties before experiencing motherhood. My mom needed to calm down because she could be assured that she didn't fail in that area.

CHAPTER EIGHTEEN
TY

Crystal's father wasn't too bad. If I had a daughter, I would be asking the same questions. I didn't blame him for wanting to check me out, but I just wished I was really the average guy. Although I would be seventeen soon, I was far more mature than the average sixteen year old, due to the type of life I live. I didn't lie to Crystal's father. I promised to protect her and with my life if need be.

Crystal walked back in just as I was about to leave. "Go ahead and walk your young man out," Mr. Jackson said. "One other thing before you go."

"Sir?" I asked, looking him in the eyes.

"I don't want y'all sneaking around. If you want to see my daughter, you can see her here within reasonable hours."

"Yes, sir."

"Enjoy the rest of your day," Crystal's father said. She and I walked out the front door. I grabbed Crystal's hand as soon as the door shut and kissed the back of it.

"I knew you were special the first day I laid eyes on you."

Crystal looked up at me and smiled. "I think you're special too, Ty."

My heart skipped a beat or two. "I hadn't planned on telling you this, this soon since we really haven't known each other long, but I can't go another moment without letting you know that you're my heart. I love you."

Tears flowed down Crystal's face. I wiped them away with my fingers. "Can you say that again?" she asked.

"I love you."

"I love you too, Ty. I love you so much."

I kissed Crystal gently on the lips and then squeezed her tight. I held her in my arms and never wanted to let go. Our hearts beat in sync. I kissed her on top of her forehead and then pulled away. "I better get going before your dad comes out here with his shotgun." We both laughed.

I watched Crystal walk back inside. Reluctantly, I walked back across the street to JC's house. JC was sitting at the table eating, so I made me a plate and joined him. I told him about my day.

"I got the money and the note you left," JC said in between bites. "What's up with that?"

"That's the least I can do. Your mom's gonna get tired of me eating up her food," I said after taking the last bite of potato salad from my plate.

"As long as you keep putting money in her pockets, she won't be complaining." JC took a big gulp of his drink.

"Man, I got to find a place to stay. I'm getting tired of that little old bed, and besides, you need your space."

JC shrugged. "Man, it's on you. You can stay here as long as you need to. I'm not asking you to leave."

"And I appreciate that, man. It's good to know that I have at least one person I can trust other than my brother."

"And Crystal," JC added.

I smiled. "Aw man. Crystal. That girl there is my heart."

"I know, man. Sorry, I kind of gave you a hard time about her at first. I can tell you love her."

"But man, this situation with my brother got me worried. I don't want no trouble coming your way and definitely don't want Crystal in harm's way."

JC looked in the direction of his weapon he kept nearby. "You know I'm good. Somebody will have to go through both of us to get to Crystal."

"I knew you would have my back," I responded.

"I heard about the drive-by this morning, but you know that's bound to happen in the Big D."

"True, but still, I don't know if they were trying to send a message to my brother, or if it was just random."

"Oh, speaking of your brother. This came today." JC got up from where he was sitting and returned with a big brown box with no return address.

I took the box and went to the bathroom for privacy. I turned to close the door and saw JC standing at the end of the hallway. Once inside of the bathroom, I placed the box on the sink and used my strength to remove the tape from the box. Inside the box were several items. On top was a letter. I recognized the handwriting as my brother's. I removed the letter from the envelope and read it to myself.

If you're reading this letter, this means my life is in jeopardy. If you don't hear from me within forty-eight hours after receiving the contents of this box, lil bro, I need you to take the contents along with the item I gave you to the Feds. Don't take no chances. I don't want you to follow in my footsteps. There's enough money in the safe deposit box for you to live off. Concentrate on school and make something of yourself. You're smart with numbers. Be an accountant or something. Don't be like your older brother. A fool who stayed in the game too long. Well, time is short and I got to get out of here. Love you and I know you love me too. Don't worry. Regardless of the outcome, know that I lived a good life. Dangerous but good. Let me go before I get all mushy on you.
Love M.

Fortunately, JC wasn't around because tears filled my eyes as I sat down on the toilet seat and read the letter over and over.

CHAPTER NINETEEN
CRYSTAL

Dear Diary,

Ty told me he loves me. Can you believe it? He loves me just like I love him. I'm so happy right now that I can burst. Now I know how the characters in my mom's romance novels feel. I never want this feeling to end.

But my mom, she's tripping big time. She's talking about putting me on birth control. I'm not even thinking about sex. Can't I just enjoy being in love right now? Ty and Crystal. Crystal and Ty. I like how our names click. We go together like peanut butter and jelly.

"Crystal, what's going on with you? You don't answer your phone. Return texts. If we're going to get our group Adore back on track, we need full cooperation from everybody," Dena stated the next day at school when she saw me in the hallway.

"I got a lot going on," I responded.

"Do you still want to do this, or did you change your mind?" Dena asked.

"I'm in for sure."

"So what's going on? Sade said you weren't talking to her either."

"It's only been what—two days since I haven't talked to either of you. Give me a freaking break."

Dena grabbed my arm and pulled me to the side. "Chris. We're concerned about you."

"I'm fine, okay. Look, I got to go. Meet me at lunch and I'll tell you everything," I said.

Normally, I would tell my two best friends everything, but these last few days my life had been consumed with Ty and the drama at home.

At lunchtime, I couldn't enter the lunch room without Dena waving her arms up and down trying to flag me down. I got my lunch and slipped in the seat across from her.

"Spill it," Dena blurted. She didn't give me time to say grace over my food. I ignored her and did just that. I added mustard to the hot dog before I even addressed Dena.

"I have a boyfriend."

"A what? Is it the dude you were telling me about?" she asked. Dena drank from her juice.

"Yes, the one and the same. He loves me, and Dena, I feel the same way about him."

"Chris, you just met this dude. I told you he's a drug dealer."

"I know all I need to know about Ty. He's not the bad person you're making him out to be."

"I didn't say he was a bad person. I just don't think you should be falling all in love with him because of what he does," Dena said.

"He's only doing it because he has to." I found myself defending Ty.

"I'm only saying this because I love you. You're like a sister to me, and I don't want to see you get caught up in that life."

"You're one to talk. Your boyfriend sold drugs."

"I know, and that's why I know you're not cut out to be a drug dealer's girlfriend. You got to deal with watching your back, his back, and don't forget the girls always throwing themselves at him."

"I'm not worried about any of that," I lied.

"You don't know what you're getting yourself into."

"Look. Either you're going to be supportive, or you can keep your comments about Ty to yourself. I will not sit here and listen to you bash my man. Anyway, I thought you were cool with me hooking up with Ty."

"I was. But the more I think about it, I don't think it's in your best interest," Dena responded.

Tired of listening to Dena, I left my half-eaten hotdog on the tray and left Dena talking to herself. I threw my food in the trash and headed to my next class. I refused to let Dena's negativity put a shadow over my happiness.

When I saw Dena later in the hallway, I turned my back to her. She spoke, but I didn't. I really didn't want to hear anything else she had to say. I pulled out my cell phone and sent Ty a text message. Before I could get to my next class I received a response back. I smiled when I pulled up the graphics with a rose and heart saying I love you. I replied with a smiley face and typed in the words 'I love you' right before turning my phone off.

The rest of the day dragged on. I was looking for my cell phone when I accidentally bumped into Dena. "Sorry," I said and kept walking toward the curb.

"Crystal, we need to talk."

"If it's about Ty, we don't have anything to talk about."

"I'm sorry, okay? I'm happy that you're in love." Dena held out her hands to hug me.

I didn't want her to look stupid, so I hugged her. "I know you're just saying it to appease me, but that's fine. Once you get to know him, you'll like him too."

"I'm sure he's a cool guy."

"He really is. There he is now. Come on. I'll introduce y'all." I grabbed Dena, and we walked up to the SUV. I opened the door. "Ty, this is my best friend Dena." They exchanged greetings. I sat down in the front seat and closed the door.

Ty said, "Dena, if you like, I can drop you off at home."

Dena looked back at the crowded bus and then back at us. "Sure. Don't have to ask me twice." Ty unlocked the back door. Dena climbed in the backseat.

"Where to?" Ty asked her.

Dena spouted out her address. Ty turned the music down as Dena and I talked about our group Adore.

Ty asked, "So when will I get a chance to hear this CD?"

Dena said, "I'm so glad you asked. I never go anywhere without a copy. Give it back to Crystal when you finish listening to it." Dena handed him a copy of our CD.

Ty immediately put the CD in and started playing it. Dena and I sang along as it played. Ty seemed to be enjoying the music.

"My girlfriend is going to be a star," he said with a proud look on his face.

"You know it. Now, don't be one of those jealous dudes trying to hold a sister back," Dena said. I wanted to reach behind me and pop her in the mouth.

Ty responded, "Oh, my baby has my full support. I will do whatever I can to make sure she's a success."

I smiled, turned, and did something childish. I licked my tongue out at Dena. She kept any other smart comments she may have had to herself.

"Thanks for the ride," Dena said when Ty dropped her off.

"No problem," Ty responded.

"I'll talk to you later," I said as she walked away.

As soon as we pulled off, I said, "Sorry about Dena. She can sometimes be a little outspoken."

"Oh. No, she's cool. She's just watching out for her girl. I can't do nothing but respect that," Ty responded.

"Enough about Dena. Do you really like the CD?" I asked.

"I'm glad I met you now, because once you blow up you might not have time for me."

I leaned over and kissed him on the cheek. "Baby, I will always have time for the love of my life." I meant it too. Ty was the love of my life and nothing would separate us.

CHAPTER TWENTY
TY

I stopped going to school because my mind wasn't on class, but I made sure I was available to pick up Crystal every day. Almost forty-eight hours went by and still no word from my brother. It was a moonless night, pitch black, except the one streetlight and the light from my cell phone.

An unknown number displayed across the screen. I answered the phone without it having to ring twice. "Ty, I need you to listen and listen good. Do not trust anybody. Nobody is who they seem," Michael said.

"Where are you, man?" I asked.

"I'm safe. That's all you need to know. My boy Jay turned on me. He tried to set me up with Slick. I had t-t-t-to…" Michael stuttered. "I had to kill my best friend."

Things went from bad to worse. Jay and Michael were like brothers. Closer probably than him and I were. I knew it had to tear him up inside. "What happened?" I asked.

"He wanted to take over my territory, so he was feeding Slick information about me. That's why Slick started looking at me sideways. I'm so glad I didn't tell him about my deal."

"Are you sure he doesn't know?" I had my doubts.

"No, I'm not. That's another reason why I'm in hiding. But after they find Jay and some of his bodyguards dead, I'm sure I'm going to be number one on their suspect list. I need you to be extra careful until things blow over."

"When will I hear from you again?" I asked.

"I'll try to contact you tomorrow. If more than twenty-four hours pass and you don't hear from me. Follow the directions in that letter."

"You sure you want to do it. We got enough money. We can get up out of this town and start life somewhere else," I said.

"No, man. I'm in this too deep."

I tried to keep Michael on the phone. The longer I talked to him, the more I knew he was all right. "What do you want me to tell Mom?" I asked.

"I sent her a package. Go by and check to make sure she got it. Be discreet though," Michael said.

"Oh, you know I know how to keep tails off me."

"Lil bro, I got to go. Wish I had more time to talk, but I need to get back to my hiding place. Where I'm at now, the cell signal is bad."

"Love you, man," I said.

"Love you too, lil bro," he responded, right before disconnecting the call.

Although it was late in the day, I needed to see my mom. I needed to feel her caring arms around me. After I informed JC that I was leaving, I hopped in my SUV and made sure I wasn't being tailed. I drove directly to my mom's condo in north Dallas. The light was still on in the living room, so I knew she was still up. I parked right in front.

I jumped out of the truck and rang the doorbell. The door opened and there she stood. All five-foot five-inches of her wearing a pink robe and a hairnet. She looked absolutely beautiful. "Come on in, boy. I was wondering when I was going to see you." Mom hugged me so tight that I didn't want to let go. She released me and I moved inside as she closed the front door.

"Mama, I missed you."

"You boys should make your way over to see me more. I know you have your own lives, but still," she complained.

"I know, Mama. Things have just been hectic."

She sat down on the sofa, picked up the remote, and turned the volume down to her favorite late night show, The David Letterman Show. "You know I love you because you're making me miss Letterman's monologue."

"Yes, Mama," I said, sounding more like a six year old than a sixteen year old.

"Your brother done gone and got himself caught up in some mess, I see," she said.

One thing about my mama. She'd never been one to bite her tongue. I wasn't sure what Michael had revealed to her, so I kept my mouth shut. She went on and on about what she knew. Apparently, she knew more than I thought. "Why don't you move back in with me?" she asked.

"Mom, you know I can't do that."

"I know no such thing. Your brother told me you were getting out of that life. You need to, or you're going to end up just like him. He's left enough money for you to do that."

"I didn't realize you knew what we did."

"Boy, I might be old, but I'm not stupid. Your brother is only doing what your daddy taught him to do."

Did she just mention our dad? She normally didn't mention him to me. Every time I would bring it up in the past, she would pretend like she didn't hear me. "What did you say?"

"You heard me. Your dad was a dope dealer. How do you think Michael got in the business?"

"But Mama, you told me dad left us. Are you telling me he's been around all this time?"

Mama got up and poured herself a drink. "I knew this day would come, and I had hoped I would never have to tell you."

I squeezed the pillow on the sofa in order to direct my frustration somewhere. "Mom, spill it. The suspense is killing me."

She sipped her drink and sat beside me. Then she reached for my hand and squeezed it. "You were too young to remember this. Every time we moved, someone would shoot up our house. The last time it happened, I got you boys and ran and hid. I couldn't go back home because my mama didn't want me. I got on government assistance and got us in that run-down house you probably remember growing up in. I didn't care that it was run down. It was something we could call home, and it was safe. Safe from your dad and safe from the people who always seemed to want him dead."

"So you knew where my dad was all of this time?" I was in complete shock. My mom had lied to me. This was a little too much to take in.

"I knew, but I tried to keep him away from you because I knew he was a bad influence. He would send money, but I would send it right back. I moved again. This time to a better house, and I thought he didn't know where we were. Wrong."

"Mom, thanks for the history lesson, but get to the point. Where is my daddy?"

"Boy, show some respect. I'm getting to that. Michael came home and told me about this man in a black Cadillac giving him money and candy every day after school who claimed to be his godfather. I caught a glimpse of the dude, but knew before I saw him that it was your dad." She paused while she refilled her drink of choice. A glass of bourbon. "By then your father was a big time dope dealer. Not too many people were crazy enough to shoot at him. The Cadillac was just one of many of his cars. I did the best that I could with you boys, but times were hard. Michael, being as stubborn as your daddy, felt the need to be the man of the house, so he started slanging. I tried to stop him at first, but he wouldn't stop. When he wanted to set me up in this house to get away from the old neighborhood, I jumped at the chance. I couldn't stand by and watch my boys turn out just like their no good father."

I clenched my fists as I listened. My patience ran thin. "Who is he?" I asked.

"Samuel Davis is your daddy."

"Where is my daddy now?"

"Tyreek, you know exactly where he is."

"No, I don't. If I did, I wouldn't be asking you."

"Slick. Slick's your daddy, son."

I stared at my mom in total disbelief. "You got to be kidding me," I responded.

"I hate to be the bearer of bad news, but yes, it's true." She gulped down the rest of her drink.

Upset, I got up and started pacing back and forth in front of the couch. I cursed out loud, not caring that my mom could hear me. I wanted to punch a hole in something. She got up and rested her hand on my shoulder. Her gentle touch calmed me.

"I understand your anger. Don't be mad at me. Please don't be mad at him. I did what I thought was best, but you guys still ended up following in his footsteps." I saw the sincere look of regret in my mom's eyes. My anger at her dissolved itself. But as far as Slick went. No. He knew he was my dad, so he should have said something. I rushed out of the house. My mom didn't follow me. Frustrated and upset, I sent Michael a text message. I didn't know how long I sat in the SUV before starting the engine up. I banged the steering wheel hard and sped off toward the freeway.

CHAPTER TWENTY-ONE
CRYSTAL

You would think for a Saturday, the clinic wouldn't be full but it was. I watched my mom fill out paperwork. The receptionist informed my mom that we got there just in time because they were about to stop taking appointments. She handed my mom some brochures. My mom glanced down at them and then handed them to me.

"Read these while I fill out these forms."

I did as instructed. The pamphlets were about sexually transmitted diseases and practicing safe sex. It also gave statistics on the rate of teen pregnancies and the dangers of having a baby at such an early age.

My mom didn't have to worry. I didn't want any babies until I was married. I finished reading the brochures and glanced around the room. Some of the girls here were pregnant already. I guess they came in a little too late for birth control.

The girl next to me said, "Can you pass me that?" She pointed to a fashion magazine.

I handed it to her. "Here you go."

"Thanks," she responded. "So your mom dragged you down here?" she asked.

"Yes. For a regular checkup, I guess."

"Most of us are here for birth control or refill on medicine."

"Medicine for what?" I asked.

My mom looked at me from the corner of her eye as she continued to fill out the forms.

"I'm here because my boyfriend gave me something. I knew he was sleeping with other girls. I should have been smarter and used a condom."

I shifted in my seat, wondering if what she had was contagious. My mom must have overheard the conversation because she picked up a brochure and shoved it in my hand. The brochure was filled with information about herpes. It was information from the Centers for Disease Control and Prevention. It read: There is no cure for herpes, but treatment is available to reduce symptoms and decrease the risk of transmission to a partner.

I knew AIDS was not curable, but I had no idea that herpes was also incurable. If this information was meant to scare me, it accomplished its purpose. I didn't want any disease that couldn't be cured, nor did I want a disease that could be cured. But I also didn't want a child at my young age. If it was up to me, we could have left. I was scared into not having sex, but my mom wasn't going for us leaving, so I waited. The girl I was talking to got called to the back. My mom said, "Even though I'm about to put you on birth control. If you do decide to have sex with that Ty fellow, you better make sure you use a condom."

"Mom!" I said in embarrassment and looked around to see if anyone was listening. Everyone else seemed to be in their own little world.

We were called to the back, and I nervously undressed and got up on the table. Mom said, "I'm going to be right here. It might hurt a little, but the pain won't last long."

"Oh, thanks Mom," I said and not in a pleasant voice either.

The female doctor did her best to make me feel comfortable, but there's nothing comfortable about a cold metal instrument between your legs. I shut my eyes and squeezed my mom's hands. I finally breathed when the doctor said, "Crystal, I'm finished."

I listened to the doctor talk to my mom. "We can give her a shot, or we can prescribe some pills. I suggest the shot because some of these young ladies aren't taking the pills on the right schedule."

Immediately, I pouted. I didn't want either, but it was my mom's decision. Mom looked at me. "Crystal, which one do you prefer? You're responsible, so I trust you would take the pills, but it's your choice."

Ugh. I didn't want to think about it. "I'll take the shot." I didn't want to think about taking the pill every single day.

I knew if I didn't, my mom would be on my case about it. This way if I got the shot, I wouldn't have to hear her talk about it.

The nurse handed the doctor the syringe. She pulled up the sleeve of my cloth gown and stuck the needle in my arm. "Ouch!" I said.

The doctor rubbed the spot with an alcohol pad. "It might hurt for a few days. If a bump develops, bring her back in," she informed my mom.

Once the doctor and nurse left the room, I put on my clothes. I could barely walk.

"I can rest knowing that we got that out of the way," Mom said as we entered the car.

My hand flew to the spot where I got the shot. "It still hurts."

"If the pain doesn't go away by morning let me know," Mom responded.

I thought we were going home, but instead my mom drove to the nail shop. I guess she was feeling guilty about putting me under the torture of the exam. An hour and half later, we both walked out with a manicure and pedicure. All was forgiven.

"If your dad asks, don't tell him anything. I've been working overtime. The least I could do is treat us to a mani and pedi."

I agreed. No sense in working hard and not being able to treat yourself. That was another reason why I couldn't wait for Adore to take off. The first thing I was going to do was buy my parents a house when I became rich. One of those big houses. I would throw in a maid and butler too. I could see it now. I leaned back in my seat and daydreamed about stardom as my mom drove us home.

CHAPTER TWENTY-TWO
TY

I hadn't slept since my mom revealed the identity of my father. Michael finally called me, but he was just as clueless as I was. The only good thing about it all, Michael did agree to meet me in a secret location. The chirp from my phone indicated a new incoming text. I glanced down. Michael texted the location. I made sure I wasn't being followed. I entered the address in the GPS and followed the directions. It led me to a house on the outskirts of town. It looked like the average American neighborhood. I slipped my Glock in my waist and exited the car.

Michael met me at the door. "Come in," he said, glancing outside to make sure no one else was around. He shut the door, and then grabbed me in a brotherly hug. "Missed you, man."

"Same here." I looked around the nearly empty house. The living room had a sofa and a television. Nothing more.

"We don't have much time," Michael said.

"What are we going to do about Slick?" I blurted out.

Michael paced back and forth. "I should have known. I was old enough to know he was our dad. Something in me must have blocked it out."

"It didn't help that the only picture we had was fuzzy. Thanks to Mom," I added.

"Man, I don't know what to do. The information I have on Slick that I promised the Feds can send him away a very long time."

"So what are you going to do?"

"I can't do it. I can't be responsible for sending our dad away. Slick has been good to me. Made sure I was well taken care of. I should have listened to my gut feeling when those Feds busted me and just took the time instead of turning into a snitch."

"Man, you just did what you thought was best. Don't beat yourself up."

"If we're Slick's kids, something foul is going on. Someone keeps wanting me to think Slick is the one who has been trying to harm me, but Slick wouldn't do that. Especially to his firstborn."

"Then what do you think is happening?" I asked.

"Slick better watch his back. Someone in his inner circle is trying to take him out. And they will do it by any means necessary. Somebody else besides Mama must know that I'm his son. If anything happened to Slick, I would be next in line to take over the throne, and the only person that would affect is his right hand man, Lamb."

"Lamb was the one who sent those guys to rough me up?"

"Yes, and Lamb is the one who actually kept me from talking to Slick since all of this drama started."

"Finding out that Slick is our father has knocked the wind out of me."

"Lil bro. I know the feeling." Michael stopped pacing and sat on the couch. His phone rang and he answered the call. "I'll be there in forty-five minutes." He turned and looked at me. "That's my people calling. I'm going to have to leave here shortly."

I dropped my head. "I understand."

"Where's your phone?" he asked.

I removed it from my pocket. He took it from me, entered several numbers, and then showed me the display. "This is Slick's private number. Very few people have it. When you get back into the city limits, call the number and talk to him only. Tell him you need to see him and it's urgent."

"What am I to tell him? I don't want to see him by myself. I don't know how I'll react," I said.

"Look, Ty, I need you to do this for me. When you see him face to face, let him know you want to talk to him in private. That it's about a life insurance policy your mom left."

"But he knows our mom isn't dead, if he's our father."

"Exactly, but nobody else does. When you tell him that, he'll know something is up and he'll have the place cleared. When he does, you need to text me and I will call you. When you do that, hand him the phone and I'll take over from there."

"But, man, I don't know. I don't know if I'll be able to face Slick knowing that he's our dad."

Michael patted me on the shoulder. "You can and you will. You must. You must do it for all of our safety. Trust me when I say this. Lamb is the last person that should be in control of Slick's empire. Slick shows mercy. Lamb is merciless."

I agreed. I'd heard stories about Lamb, and from Michael's expression, all I'd heard was true. "Okay, I'll do it."

"Do it as soon as possible. Make sure you're available to meet with him whatever day and time he says. The sooner the better."

"Got it," I responded as Michael walked me to the door.

"Stay strapped and be careful." He gave me another hug.

"Strapped for life," I responded.

Back outside, I jumped in my car and headed to the city limits of Dallas.

CHAPTER TWENTY-THREE
CRYSTAL

I had been calling and texting Ty, but he wasn't returning any of my messages. I listened to Hope sing a song out of tune for her school play. Talent was not part of her DNA for sure, but me being the good older sister that I am, said, "Crystal, let me help you with the song. You need to stop sounding like you're holding your breath." I worked with Hope and used some of the techniques my choir teacher at school taught me. By the end of the afternoon, Hope sounded a lot better. She wasn't another me, but at least now I didn't need a pair of earplugs to drown her out.

"That's so sweet to see you helping out your little sister," my mom said as she watched from the doorway of Hope's room.

"Anything to stop her from sounding like a screeching cat," I said.

Hope rolled her eyes and stuck out her tongue. "All of us aren't in a singing group," she blurted.

"What's this I hear about a singing group?" My mom walked further into the room.

Before I could say anything, Hope pulled out a CD from under her pile of things and handed it to Mom. I wanted to wring her little neck. "She's in this group called Adore." Hope smiled while crossing her arms.

Mom looked at me and then back at the CD. "Looks like you're full of surprises. Let me check this out. See what my daughter is working with. We might have a star on our hands."

"Sade's singing lead on most of the songs. I only have one lead," I confessed.

"Which number is that?" Mom asked. She sincerely showed interest in what I had going on, which is something that hadn't happened in over a year.

"It's number seven. The song is called 'Sweet Love of Mine.'"

"Mmm. Huh. I wonder who inspired that song?" Her eyebrow lifted.

"Uh, Mom, I didn't even know Ty then."

"That's what your mouth says. Well, let me listen to this and I'll tell you what I think." She walked over to Hope's stereo and put the CD in. I watched her facial expression change. I wasn't sure if she liked the song or not.

"So what do you think?" I asked after she turned it off.

Mom walked up and hugged me. "My baby's going to be a star. We got to get y'all some cute outfits. Get you on some shows. I need to get my hair done. I can't be looking any kind of way."

"Slow down, Mom. The CD won't be out just yet. In about another month. Dena's cousin is our manager, so she's set us up to be an act at the Summer Jam."

Hope's eyes lit up. "Are you serious? Everybody that's anybody is going to be there. Can't believe you all are going to be there."

"Yes, I'm serious," I responded.

"I haven't seen you girls rehearsing. You can't get out there and half way do things. Y'all should be rehearsing every day," Mom said. She seemed just as excited as I was when I first heard.

"We've been trying to give Sade a little time since she lost the baby and with the move."

"The move? What are you talking about?"

"Oh, you didn't know. Ms. Joyce is moving them to north Dallas."

"That heifer ain't told me nothing." Mom grabbed Hope's cell phone. It was locked. "What's the code to unlock your phone?"

"Mom. That's a secret," Hope responded.

"Last time I checked, I was the one who bought you the phone. Code please."

Hope reluctantly whispered the code to her. My mom entered it and dialed a number. "Joyce, this Maddie. Why did I have to learn about you moving from my daughter?" Mom left Hope's room.

Hope pouted. "I hope she doesn't forget whose phone that is."

"You better hope she doesn't hear you."

"Oh, and I know you hid your diary. I'm going to find it," Hope said as I was getting ready to leave her room.

"And if I catch you reading it, your behind is mine. And I will show you no mercy."

The doorbell rang. Mom was still on the phone with Ms. Joyce. Our dad was out with some friends of his, so I went to the front door and peeked in the peephole first. I opened the door with a frown on my face.

"Baby, I know you've been calling me all day, but I had a lot going on," Ty said.

"Hi. I'm Crystal's little sister, Hope," Hope said from behind me before I could even say anything.

Ty, being the nice person that he is, spoke to Hope. Me, I ignored her. "Come on. Let's go outside, so we can have some privacy." I looked back at Hope as I said it. I closed the door and we took a seat on the steps. "This better be good," I said. "It doesn't take but a second to respond to a text."

"I know, but I've been driving. I saw my brother today."

I forgot about being angry. "Are you serious? Is he okay?"

"Yes and no."

I listened to Ty explain about finding out who his father was. I wanted to pull him into a hug and never let go. The sound of his voice cracking let me know this situation was really tearing him up.

"How do I let him know I know who he is, or should I even tell him?" Ty asked.

I really didn't have a solution, but he was looking for me to give him an answer. I closed my eyes and then opened them. "Do what your heart leads you to do," I responded.

"My heart is all confused. For years I've held resentment toward him for abandoning us, but now I know he didn't do that . . ."

"Have you tried to reach out to him?" I asked.

"Yes. We're meeting up tomorrow."

"Cool. If you need me to go with you, I can."

"No, this is something I have to do myself. But I really appreciate you volunteering to be by my side. It really means a lot to me to know that you have my back like this."

"We're the new age Bonnie and Clyde. Where ever you ride, I ride," I responded.

Ty leaned over and our lips locked into a long kiss.

CHAPTER TWENTY-FOUR
TY

JC gave me my much needed space as I contemplated what to wear. What did one wear when going to meet their father officially for the first time? I got clearance to meet with Slick at one, and I didn't want to be late. I opted to wear a pair of jeans and a Dallas Cowboys jersey with a matching hat. I put on the latest Jordans and left JC's house. I glanced over at Crystal's house. I had hoped to run into her before leaving, but she wasn't back from church. I sent her a quick text to let her know I was about to go see my dad. One thing I left out last night when opening up to Crystal was the fact that Slick was my dad. I also sent Michael a quick text, so he would be expecting another text once I'd spoken with our father by myself.

Ironically, the song, "Stuntin' Like My Daddy" by Lil Wayne and Birdman was on K104 as I drove toward Slick's estate. I turned the air conditioner to high as sweat poured from my forehead. The closer I got to Slick's place, the more nervous I felt. I pulled up to the gate. Two armed guards approached. One on each side of my vehicle. I rolled down my window. One asked, "Who are you here to see?"

I felt like I had a frog in my throat. I cleared my throat. "Slick."

The guard on the right side said, "He knows you're coming?"

"Yes. I talked to him yesterday."

"What's your name?" the guard on the driver's side asked me.

"I'm Doughboy."

"I don't see a Doughboy on here." The guard looked at his pad.

"Tyreek," I said.

"Oh, yeah. There's a Tyreek on here. Man, he good. Open the gates," the guard said as he used his arm to motion to the other guard.

The second guard walked back to the booth and hit a button. The black iron gate opened.

"You can park anywhere except in the spot with a name painted on the ground."

"Okay," I responded as I slowly drove through the gates.

I'd never been to Slick's estate. It looked like one of those places out of a movie. The house was probably at least a mile away from the road as I yielded to the right and drove on the circular driveway. I admired the beautiful flowers as I found a parking spot. There were only a few cars other than Slick's, so hopefully, I would have the privacy I needed to talk to him.

I parked my SUV and hopped out. While walking past several huge golden statues of lions, I stopped and checked one out. I wanted to touch one, but was afraid that Slick would have my hand cut off if they were watching me on a security camera. I walked up the huge stairs to the front door, still admiring the grandeur of Slick's place. I'd never seen anything like it. I rang the doorbell. A man dressed in a black tuxedo answered the door. "Master Slick is waiting for you. Follow me."

I walked past the butler and waited for him to lead me. My eyes followed the long spiral staircase to the top of the stairway. I saw several people that I didn't know looking down at me.

"This way," the older man said.

"Coming," I stated as I increased my pace to keep up with him.

The pictures on the wall looked like the ones seen in a museum. Slick's place made the houses on MTV Cribs look like shacks.

"Master Slick, your guest is here," the black man who reminded me of Jeffrey from the Fresh Prince of Bel Air announced.

Slick's back was to me. Several men, one being Pork, were seated on the brown leather sofa. Slick was dressed in black slacks and a white, crisp dress shirt with a colorful tie. When he turned, our eyes locked.

"Young blood, welcome to my castle." Slick got up and walked toward me.

"Thank you, Slick, for taking the time to see me," I responded, keeping eye contact. He extended his hand and I shook it.

"Your mom must have raised you right. You know how to show respect," he said.

"Yes, sir. My mom did."

Slick turned to the men in the room. "Sir. See, this boy has some good home training. Unlike a lot of these young dudes around here." Slick patted me on the back. "Come and have a seat. What did you want to see me about? Do you want to get more involved in the business?"

"I wanted to talk to you about my mom's life insurance policy," I responded.

Slick had a stricken look on his face. "Son, what are you talking about?"

We were close enough where I could whisper and no one else could hear. "I need to talk to you alone." I looked over at the other men who appeared to be talking amongst themselves, but I couldn't take any chances. I didn't want them to overhear anything. Just as Michael instructed, I attempted to get Slick alone.

Slick looked at me. I didn't break the stare. He raised one of his hands in the air. "Everybody out. I need to talk to this young man in private so I can see where his head's at."

The men mumbled amongst themselves. Apparently, they weren't moving fast enough for Slick. "I said out!" he shouted. This time they jumped up out of their seats and headed toward the door. "And shut the door," Slick said.

Pork was the last to leave. He shut the door. Slick walked to the door and clicked the lock on it. He turned back around and we were again face to face and alone.

CHAPTER TWENTY-FIVE
CRYSTAL

I filled up pages and pages in my diary about my feelings for Ty. I was nervous for him because this was the day he was going to meet his father. I couldn't even imagine not knowing my dad. As much as my parents made me upset, I guess I was lucky to have both of my parents.

"Dena and Sade are here," my mom yelled from down the hall.

Before I could get up off the bed, they were walking into my room. I sat up and placed my diary under my pillow.

"What's up, ladies?" I asked.

"I talked to Sade, and she's ready to get back to rehearsing," Dena responded.

Sade plopped down at the end of my bed. "I know it's time for me to stop feeling sorry for myself. The doctor said what I'm feeling is natural. I think it'll help if I did this. It'll take my mind off everything."

It was good to see my best friend slowly coming back around to her normal self. We were busy talking about our CD when my mom stuck her head in the door. "Girls, I want you to know if you need help picking out outfits I used to be a fashionetta."

"Mom!" I said. She was trying to be cool, but it wasn't working.

"I got some ideas. If Beyoncé's mom can dress her, then I know I can dress you girls."

She did have a point. I guess I would ease up on her a little. "Fine. What do y'all say?" I looked at Dena and then at Sade.

"I think it's great. Thanks, Ms. Maddie," Sade responded.

As soon as my mom was gone, Sade said, "Forget Adore for a minute. Why am I the last person to know that you have a boyfriend?"

I gave Dena the evil eye. I planned on telling Sade, but I just hadn't gotten around to doing so. "What had happened w-w-was," I stuttered.

"I hear he's a drug dealer too. Girl, what are you getting yourself into?" Sade asked.

I rolled my eyes. "First of all, what he does has nothing to do with how he treats me and how he feels about me. Besides, there's more to Ty than what people think."

"I don't want you to get hurt. We got this group. We about to blow up. You don't need his kind of drama," Sade said.

"Sounds like you and Dena have been doing a lot of talking." I pouted.

Dena said, "We're only trying to look out for our girl."

"I'm fine. Ty loves me and I love him. That's all."

"But you just met him. How can you be in love with him already?" Sade asked.

"Love has no time limit. It is what it is," I said with conviction.

"I guess," Dena said.

"Well, that, I can agree on. I never thought I could love someone with all I've been through, but I love Brandon," Sade said.

"Brandon's a good guy," Dena said.

"So is Ty," I said, hating that my friends didn't like him. "If you got the chance to know him, you would see that he is a good guy too."

"Maybe," Dena said.

Sade remained quiet.

I was tired of talking about Ty, especially since neither one really had anything good to say. "Are we going to rehearse or what?" I asked as I got up off the bed.

I located our CD and put it in the CD player. Dena got up out of her chair and moved it to the side. We spent the next few hours rehearsing.

Practice went well. Adore was going to rock the house at the Summer Jam. All we needed were outfits. Since my mom volunteered to take care of that, we were good to go. I couldn't believe it. My life was about to change. I had always wondered how people got their start. Did they feel like I do?

After rehearsal, Sade asked, "Can you turn on your computer? There's something I want to show you."

I logged on to my computer and got on the Internet. I got up and let Sade sit down. "Brandon thought he would put this together. Check it out."

"Wow!" Dena said.

"This is great," I said as I admired the website filled with various photos of us.

"Brandon said that we needed a website, so he started this fan page."

"Oh my goodness! We already got some hits," Dena noticed.

"It's official. I'll make us a Facebook page," I said.

"Already done," Sade said. She clicked on another webpage and pulled up a Facebook Fan page.

"Two thousand fans!" Dena screamed.

"And it's growing more and more each day. It's only been up a few days," Sade said.

Regardless of our differences about Ty, we were all on one accord about Adore. We were all ready to see how far

Adore would take us. Adore was a dream come true, and I wanted to savor and enjoy each moment of it.

CHAPTER TWENTY-SIX
TY

Slick received an emergency call, so he left me alone in the room. I watched Scarface on the flat screen TV and waited. I must have dozed off because I felt a gentle shake. "Ty, wake up," Slick said.

I almost jumped out of my skin. I wiped my eyes and sat up straight. "Sorry, I fell asleep." I shifted in my seat.

"You can remain seated," Slick said. He sat in the big leather chair, picked up the remote, and turned the volume down on the television. I watched him pick up a cigar out of a box and light it. He puffed on it and then blew out smoke rings. Some of his mannerisms reminded me of Michael. I guess if I had been around Slick more, I would have picked up on the fact that he was our father.

"So tell me, son. Why did you want to see me?"

I pushed my nervousness aside. I'd always imagined what I would say when I came face to face with my father. Now that the day was here, I couldn't remember any of the words. I took a deep breath. "Slick, I appreciate you seeing me."

"You remind me of myself when I was your age," he said as he puffed on the cigar.

"I know. I know that you're Samuel Davis. The same Samuel Davis that's my father." I stared him directly in the eyes without blinking.

Slick choked on the cigar smoke and coughed several times. "Who told you that?" he asked. He got up and poured himself a drink. Ironically, it was a glass of bourbon. It seemed like he and my mom had the same drink choice.

"Your ex-wife. My mom," I finally responded.

Slick sat back down. He placed the half-empty glass and the bottle of bourbon on the table. "I can't believe this. She did her best to keep me out of your lives, and now she wants you to know that I'm your father. She's not dying, is she?" he asked. I could hear concern in his voice.

"No. So much stuff has been going on that she finally felt the need to come clean with me. But I have a question for you. Why didn't you tell me?"

Slick had a faraway look in his eyes as he spoke. "I loved your mom, but this life took her away from me. I don't blame her for leaving and wanting better for her boys. I wanted better for you and your brother too." My breath seemed to get caught up in my chest. "It hurt me to let you all go, but I could see what it was doing to your mother, so I vowed to step away. I tried to send money to help out, but your mom being the proud woman that she is wouldn't take it."

"But when my brother started working for you, you could have told us then," I blurted.

"And have to deal with your mom's wrath. I would rather fight twenty of the baddest men than deal with her when she's like that."

I knew exactly what he meant. My mom rarely got angry, but when she did she was like a roaring tornado, anything in her way would be destroyed. "You say you didn't want this type of life for us, but yet, Michael worked for you."

"That's only because I saw him hustling on the street. If I wouldn't have taken him under my wings, one of those dope boys would have took him out. I couldn't have my son out there like that. I took him in to protect him. To at least give him a way to provide for you and your mom."

"I don't know what to say to you right now," I admitted. "All of this is a shock."

"Son, I understand. I wish I could change things, but I can't."

I squinted. It really looked like Slick had tears forming in the corner of his eyes. Slick turned away, but I saw the tears when they fell down his cheeks anyway. He pulled himself together and cleared his throat. "I want you to stop selling and get your education. I hear you're a beast on the football field. You have what, one more year. Let that year count, son."

Man, I wished I had time to play catch up with him. I wished going back to school and getting back on the football team were as easy as they sounded. I wished a lot of things. I pulled out my cell phone and sent a text message to Michael.

"Slick, there's something else I came here to talk to you about."

"My son has my boldness. I love that. Although I didn't help raise you, you have some of my ways."

I didn't know if it was meant to be a compliment or not. Nor did I have much time to think about it because my cell phone rang. I answered when Michael's number popped up. "Yes, he's right here," I responded and looked at Slick. "Michael wants to talk to you."

"Where has he been? He's been M.I.A."

"He'll tell you." I handed him my phone.

I don't know what Michael was telling Slick, but most of it wasn't good. I saw Slick's facial expression change. He clenched his fist as he listened.

"I would never send anyone after you. Son, I got a lot to think about. If what you're telling me is true, I don't know who I can trust anymore."

Someone knocked and I turned toward the door. Slick said, "See who that is?"

I got up and went to the door. Pork stood in the doorway. "You still here?" he asked.

"Yes, and what do you want?" I asked as I stared at Pork without blinking.

"I need to see the boss man. We have a situation."

"He's busy right now," I said.

"Kid, you better move out of my way. When did you become his spokesman?"

Slick had slipped up behind me. "Pork, whatever it is, handle it. I have another situation I'm dealing with right now."

"But Boss. I really need—"

"Handle it!" Slick slammed the door in Pork's face. I could hear Pork say a few obscenities as he walked away.

Slick handed me my phone. Michael was still on the other end. "I told Slick everything he needs to know for now. I need you to do what he says. He won't let anything happen to you."

"But . . ." I said.

"No buts. Look. Somebody's been following me. I got to go."

Without another word, Michael disconnected the call. I now stood face to face with the man who was my father.

"I have a lot to digest. In the meantime, make sure you stay strapped at all times. You got my private number. Don't talk to nobody from my camp, but me. Understood?"

"Yes sir."

"Then go ahead and get out of here. I will be in touch. I got a lot of thinking to do."

Without another word, I left him alone with his thoughts.

CHAPTER TWENTY-SEVEN
CRYSTAL

"Crystal, your boyfriend is here," Hope said as she burst in my room.

In two seconds, I jumped off my bed and glanced at my appearance in the mirror. I picked up the brush, pulled my hair back in a ponytail, and licked my dry lips. Not satisfied with the look, I retrieved my favorite lip-gloss out of my backpack and put some on. I was so happy to see my man standing at the front door. No words were said. We embraced each other. Ty hung on to me tight as if his life depended on it.

My mother cleared her throat. "Uh, hello Ty."

Ty stopped hugging me. "Hello, Mrs. Jackson."

"Have you eaten anything? We still have some food left over from dinner," she said.

"Oh, I'm good. I'm not hungry."

"I made a pound cake."

Ty licked his lips. "Well, I could use a slice of cake."

"Crystal, go cut Ty a piece of cake. Ty, follow me." I watched my mom lead Ty to the living room. I tried my best to rush and cut him a slice of cake because I didn't want to leave him too long with my mom. They were both laughing when I returned holding the cake on the saucer.

"Where's his drink?" my mom asked.

"You just said bring him a piece of cake," I responded.

Mom stood up. "I tell you. When you want something done right, you have to do it yourself. I'll be right back." She left out of the living room. I handed Ty the saucer before taking a seat next to him.

"Oh my goodness. This is so good," he said after he took a bite.

Mom returned with a soda. "Here you go. Crystal, put a coaster on the table please."

I did as instructed. Ty drank from the soda before placing it on the coaster.

"I'm going to leave you two alone. Ty, it's good seeing you," Mom said.

I watched Ty devour the cake. "You want some more?"

"No, I'm good." He placed the empty saucer on the table. "I saw my dad today."

"How did it go?" I asked.

"Still hard to tell."

"Are you okay with everything?" I placed my hand on his knee. He squeezed my hand.

"I thought he didn't want me. To find out he only left me alone out of respect for my mom. It's just a lot to digest. A part of me is angry at my mom from denying me my dad, but I guess under the circumstances, I understand."

He may have understood, but I didn't. I bit my tongue because I didn't want to say anything that sounded like I was disrespecting his mom. "So what's next?" I asked.

"Crystal, there's something I need to tell you. I hope this doesn't change how you feel about me?" I could see the fear in his eyes when he looked at me.

"Tell me," I said with a shaky voice.

"Slick is my dad."

"Who?" I asked.

"Slick. You've heard of him, right?"

I tilted my head and tried to recall the name. Ding dong! A bell went off. "Oh, my goodness! Are you serious?"

"Yes."

Wow. I couldn't believe his dad was like Nino Brown from New Jack City. "So how does he feel about you being his son?" I asked.

"He's glad that things are finally out in the open."

I listened to Ty pour his heart out about how he felt about his dad. We curled up together on the couch and talked. I fell asleep on his shoulder. I felt his hand brush the hair off my face and woke up.

"Baby, I better get going before your mama come back in here and kick me out."

I sat up. "Yes, you better. Are you going to school tomorrow?" I asked.

"Not sure, but I will be dropping you off," Ty responded.

That night I wrote about Ty, but also about my friends in my diary. I wished they could see Ty for the type of guy he really is. Oh my goodness. When they find out Slick is his dad, they really are going to trip. If my parents find out, they are going to ban Ty from ever coming to our house. I wrote a final diary entry before placing my diary back in its hidden spot. I eased under the covers and thought of Ty as I drifted off to sleep.

The next few days were routine. I went to school, did my homework, rehearsed with the girls and talked to Ty. He seemed a little aloof, but with all he was dealing with it was understandable.

That Wednesday afternoon I had just finished my last class. Like clockwork, Ty was waiting for me by the curb when I got out of school.

"For you," Ty said as he moved his arm from behind his back and presented me with a dozen roses.

"These are beautiful." I smelled them.

"Happy anniversary, baby."

"Oh my goodness! You're right! We've been a couple for one week. So much stuff has happened. I feel like I've known you forever," I said as he opened the door.

I slid in the passenger seat and kept smelling the roses. When he got in, I leaned over and kissed him. "You make me feel so good."

"That's what I'm supposed to do. Supposed to keep a smile on my girl's face."

I smiled from ear to ear. Instead of going straight home, Ty pulled into the parking lot of Applebees. We talked and laughed over our meal. I really didn't want this evening to end. One week and it felt like Ty and I had been together for a lifetime. I loved him so much. It was the type of love I read about in my mom's romance books. It was the type of love I saw in some of the movies I watched. But this wasn't a fairytale, it was my life.

Later, Ty walked me to the front door. I turned to face him. He leaned over the roses and kissed me. "I hope you enjoyed yourself," he said as he eased back.

"I sure did," I responded, still cheesing.

"Call me after you finish your homework. Maybe we can meet outside."

"Okay." I blushed. I eased my key into the lock and walked through the door.

"I love you," I heard Ty say.

"I love you, too," I responded, and then shut the door.

CHAPTER TWENTY-EIGHT
TY

I still hadn't gone to school because with what looks like my brother and my father's life in danger, it was impossible to concentrate on school. Outside of Booker T, I sat waiting on Crystal to get out of school. I saw the sunshine of my life walk toward the car.

My phone beeped. It was a text from Michael. I was reading the text just as Crystal was getting in the car.

"Hi, baby," she said.

"Hi," I said, half paying her any attention.

My brother wanted to meet up in the same spot as before. I looked at the clock on the dashboard. I didn't have time to take Crystal home and then make it to the location. I looked out the window to see if I could see Crystal's bus. It pulled off. I hit the steering wheel.

"What's wrong?" Crystal asked.

"I need to meet my brother, but I have to do it now."

"So. I can go with you. You've met my family," Crystal said.

I didn't have time to disagree. I started the vehicle and rushed toward my brother's location. Traffic was heavy, so I had to get off and take some of the side streets.

Crystal respected the fact that I didn't want to talk, so the only sound heard in the car as I drove was music from the stereo. I pulled up behind the car that was parked out front. "Crystal, wait right here. Don't open this door for anybody but me. You hear me?" I looked at her.

With a frightened look, she responded. "Yes."

"I'm serious." I repeated myself. "In fact, just in case you need it." I removed another small caliber automatic from under the seat with a silver handle and placed it between us. "This gun is just like the one you have." I clicked the safety off.

Crystal never said a word. I opened the driver's door and then hit the lock. With my hand on my side where my gun was, I walked up to the front door. This time my brother didn't greet me. I rang the doorbell. Michael practically jerked me in the house.

"I shouldn't have had you come here. I need you to get this to Slick." He slipped me several CD cases.

"What is this?" I asked.

"Don't ask no questions. Just do what I tell you."

I was tired of being kept in the dark. Michael or somebody needed to give me some answers. "Look, Michael, I do everything you ask me to do. I ask a few questions. But what happens to you, affects me. What is going on, bro?"

Michael's phone rang. He answered it and then hung up. "You were followed."

I couldn't have been, but then again I really didn't check out my surroundings like I normally did. "Why do you say that?" I stuttered.

"You strapped?" he asked.

I pulled out my Glock. "Always."

"Good. Because you're going to need it. I need you to get ghost. Don't go back to JC's, because not even his father's reputation will be able to save you."

"My girl's in the car," I shouted.

"Come on," Michael said as we rushed out the house.

Michael reached under my car. He was holding a device when he removed his hand. "This is how they tracked us."

"I can't believe this! I should have checked."

"You didn't know, but from now on, you got to be more careful."

"I promise you I will."

"Get your girl out of here. I'm about to head underground again. Will be in touch." Without another word Michael threw the tracking device in the trash can and got in the car that was parked in front of me.

Crystal looked at me with her big doe eyes. "I thought you were going to introduce me to your brother?" she said.

"Baby girl, something came up. We need to get up out of here." I sped off behind my brother. When we got to the stop sign, I saw a black Lincoln pull into the spot I'd just left in my rearview mirror. I had a feeling it was the dudes Lamb sent. Things had just escalated to another level. I needed to get Crystal home and then find a safe spot to lay my head. I rushed through the neighborhood and saw a strange car I hadn't recognized nearby. I couldn't drop Crystal off now. If they saw her get out of my car then they would know she was with me, and there's no telling what they would do to her or her family so I drove on by. As soon as I passed them, the car sped up and hit my bumper.

Crystal bounced forward. "What in the world?"

"You all right?" I asked.

"I can't believe this is happening again," Crystal responded.

The car hit my bumper again. I looked in my rearview and saw someone extend their arm out. The next thing I saw were bullets flying.

"Baby, hold on," I said as I put the car in full gear.

People outside started ducking as I accelerated, and the people behind me kept firing. Fortunately for me, Michael made sure the vehicle was bulletproof.

"Watch out!" Crystal screamed as she held on to her seatbelt tight.

I swerved to avoid hitting a lady crossing the street. The car behind me didn't, and the woman flew up in the air.

Crystal yelled. "Oh my goodness! They hit her." She looked in her rearview mirror and I knew she saw the same terrible sight I saw. There was no way that woman made it after being tossed in the air and hitting the ground.

"Crystal, I'm going to get us to safety. I promise you," I said, tossing her my phone. "Call the first number in the call log. Put it on speaker," I ordered.

Crystal hit the speaker button. We listened as the phone rang. Michael picked up. "Lamb's people are behind me now. If this truck wasn't bulletproof we would probably be dead. I'm trying to avoid the interstate, but frankly Michael, I don't know where I'm going. My back's up against the wall, bro. I need your help. Help me save my girl."

CHAPTER TWENTY-NINE
CRYSTAL

Ty was ducking in and out of traffic while trying to dodge bullets. My cell phone rang. I was too busy trying to stay alive to answer.

Ty's brother Michael gave him instructions on where to go.

"For a moment I thought we lost them," Ty said.

"There they go!" I shouted as I saw them swerve from behind a red truck.

"Hold on," Ty stated as he hit a switch on the dashboard.

I held on for dear life as Ty seemed to be going at super turbo speed. I lost count of all the near misses of colliding with other cars. I looked behind us. The car was no longer in sight. I think I started breathing for the first time since we got tapped from behind.

Ty pulled the car behind an abandoned building. He got out first and I followed suit. He held me in his arms. "Baby, I'm so sorry for getting you in this. I need to get you home."

"I'm not going anywhere," I said.

"You have to, Crystal. The same people after my brother are now after me. I can't risk you getting hurt."

Ty used his phone and made a phone call. He talked too low for me to hear what he was saying. I leaned on the truck as he paced back and forth. I kept looking back to make sure nobody was coming. "Ty, I'm scared," I admitted.

"Baby, help is on the way. I'm going to get you away safely." Ty wrapped his arms around me. He kept a look out. We heard the roar of an engine. Ty pulled out his gun. "Get in the car," he whispered.

He didn't have to tell me twice. I jumped inside and watched him ease to the end of the building, lower his weapon, and disappear around the building. I didn't hear any gunshots, so he had to be all right. I jumped in the driver's seat just in case I would have to drive. To my surprise, Ty turned the corner and right next to him was JC.

I jumped out the truck. "JC, what are you doing here?"

"I came to rescue my two friends."

Ty said, "JC is going to make sure you get home safely."

"I'm not going anywhere." I stood and crossed my arms.

Ty pulled me close to him and looked down at me. "Baby, please don't be like this. I promise to check in with you. I will feel better if I knew you were safe."

"Fine," I said. I pulled away and started walking around the corner.

"Wait. I need to give you something," Ty said.

"Keep it." I walked around the warehouse building and got in the car JC was driving. A few minutes later, Ty and JC walked to the car. Ty opened the passenger door and handed me the silver automatic handgun.

"Take it."

"I already got one, remember?"

"Never hurts to have more than one," JC said as he got in the car.

Ty leaned down and kissed me on the forehead. "I love you. Text me when you get home."

"I'll think about it," I responded.

Ty closed the door, dropped his head, and walked away. I felt guilty for acting so mean, but I didn't want to leave. I was scared for him.

JC said, "You know he's only doing this to protect you."

I thought about it and rolled down my window. "Ty," I called out.

He stopped and turned around. "Yo."

I used my hand to signal what I was saying. "I love you too." I blew him a kiss. He blew me one back.

"We gotta go," JC said as he let up the window and pulled off.

For the first time I got a close look inside the car. JC had several weapons laid out on the seats, under the seats, and on the floor of the car. "This is a lot of stuff," I slipped and said.

"Baby girl, looks like Ty isn't the only one being followed. With the person on my tail, looks like we're going to need it. Hold on."

JC whipped the car around. My body slid and hit the passenger door. Instead of trying to get away from who was coming after us, JC drove straight toward the gray Lincoln. He rolled down his window and began to shoot.

"Grab that and be ready to hand it to me when I tell you," he said.

I ducked down in the seat and held the weapon. Did Ty actually think I would be safer with JC? I couldn't believe this. At least in the SUV the bullets bounced off. If someone shot into this car, only God could save us.

"Y'all want to play. Come on. Get some of this!" JC yelled out.

I held on to the dashboard. Neither JC nor the driver of the black car was slowing down. I closed my eyes. I thought your life was supposed to pass before your eyes in the end. Mine didn't, but I knew the end was near. JC roared up the engine and kept firing.

"Hold on!" JC yelled again.

I couldn't help but hold on. I opened my eyes, and just when I thought we were about to collide, JC jerked the steering wheel and we went to the right of the car. JC never stopped shooting.

We heard a loud boom. I sat up in my seat and turned to look around. The Lincoln had flipped over a few times.

"That'll teach them for messing with me. I'm a G, baby," JC said.

I'd never seen this side of JC, so his actions came as a big surprise. I always got the nice and quiet JC. This JC was acting like he was used to this kind of stuff.

"Just get me home, please." I put the gun down I had been holding for JC on the seat in between us.

"Ain't nothing going to happen to you on my watch, baby girl. Believe that."

I wish I had as much confidence in JC as he had in himself.

CHAPTER THIRTY
TY

Every little noise had me on edge. I got back in my car and drove to Mesquite. The lady at the front desk of the hotel looked at me funny, but her look changed when I pulled out several hundred dollar bills to pay for my room for a week. I'd actually given her more than the room would cost, so I knew she was going to pocket the rest.

"If you need anything, call me. I mean call downstairs," she said, handing me the key.

I smiled as I took it. My smile faded as soon as I turned my back. The woman was old enough to be my mama. I knew I looked older than my sixteen years, but dang. She knew I was a youngster. She'd glanced at my fake ID, and the age on there said twenty-one. She probably had grandkids my age while she was trying to push up on me.

Totally exhausted, I threw my duffle bag on one of the beds and then plopped down on the other one. I dozed off until my phone chirped. The display showed Crystal's name. I turned on my side and called her.

Crystal began blurting out what happened after she and JC left me. "Why didn't you call me?" I asked.

"We were in the mix. Didn't have time to."

How did that happen? I wondered. I needed to talk to JC. "Stay by the phone. I'm going to call you right back." I dialed JC's number. No answer. I called his house phone. His mom picked up.

"JC's not here. I haven't seen him since he left this morning," she informed me.

I called JC again on his cell phone. This time he answered. "What's up, man? Crystal told me what happened."

JC mumbled something I couldn't understand. Then I heard another voice. "Is this Doughboy?" the voice asked.

"Who is this?" I asked.

"Nigga, don't worry about who I am. You need to get your scrawny ass where I am before your friend here becomes a part of the Trinity River."

"Don't hurt him. You better not hurt him." I sat straight up in the bed.

"I think you have something that belongs to me."

"Again, who is this?" I asked.

"I'm gentle as a Lamb, but more vicious than a snake," he responded and then burst out laughing.

"What do you want from me?" I asked.

"I want you to give me the disks your brother gave you."

"I don't know what you're talking about," I lied.

"Your brother didn't give you any disks?" the man asked.

"No. Please let my friend go."

"No disks. No friend. I suggest you call your brother so we can do an even exchange."

"I don't know how to reach my brother."

"Doughboy, you're lying. We tracked you to where he was earlier."

"Thanks to you, I now have no way of contacting him."

"Look. I don't have time to play games with you, Ty. We want those disks."

This time I recognized the voice. It was loud and clear and there was no mistake. It was Lamb.

"You don't believe I will do anything. Well, listen to this."

I heard a gunshot and then JC yelled out. "Man, you didn't have to shoot my leg."

"I'll call you back in one hour. Get those disks, or the next time the bullet's going straight to the head."

JC shouted, "Don't listen to him!"

I don't know if my mind was playing tricks on me or not, but I could have sworn I heard another loud boom before the call disconnected. I couldn't leave my man out there like that. I sent Michael a text. He called me immediately. "They got JC," I said in a panic.

"Calm down. Who has him?" Michael asked.

"Lamb."

"Did you call Slick?" he asked.

"No. Lamb works for him. I still don't trust Slick."

Michael said, "Slick is one thing, but trust me when I say he doesn't like traitors. He had no clue what Lamb was up to, but now that he does, Lamb's day is coming."

"But when?" I hit the pillow. "My best friend is about to get killed, and I feel so helpless."

"What number did Lamb call from?"

I recited JC's number to Michael. "He's supposed to call me back in an hour."

"When he calls you back, get the location. I need you to call Slick on the three-way."

I dialed Slick's number. "Baby boy, good to hear from you."

I let Michael talk. "Ty has a situation. Looks like your boy Lamb has his best friend captive."

Slick cursed. "Hold on." Slick must have used another phone to call Lamb. "Where are you?" Slick asked. We couldn't hear Lamb's response. Slick went on to say, "What? Somebody's late with my money? Why are you at The Spot?" There was a pause. "Did I authorize you to do that? Do you know whose son that is? Man, I don't need that kind of heat. I suggest you let him go and hope his father forgets this ever happened."

I hoped Lamb would listen to Slick. My heart dropped when I heard Slick say, "What do you mean it's too late?" Slick cursed some more. "Meet me at my crib at eight in the morning. We're going to have an emergency meeting."

Slick came back online. "Son, I hate to be the one to tell you this, but your friend is gone."

"Gone?" I yelled. "No. It can't be. He didn't have nothing to do with this. Why they have to mess with him?" I asked over and over.

Michael attempted to calm me down, but wasn't successful. I felt like throwing the phone up against the wall. "Ty. Where are you? I'll come to where you are."

"I don't know who to trust anymore. I don't think I can trust either one of you," I said, right before hanging up the phone.

I fell back on the bed and cried like a baby at the loss of my best friend who was just like a brother to me.

CHAPTER THIRTY-ONE
CRYSTAL

"Mama, I don't feel like going," I said as she looked at me from my bedroom doorway.

"Crystal, you shouldn't have stayed up late on that doggone computer. You're going to school and that's final, so I suggest you get your behind up and get dressed so you won't miss your bus." She paused and then said, "And just in case you dilly dally around and miss the bus. I'll leave five dollars on the kitchen counter for the city bus."

I fell back on my pillow. "Ugh." I really didn't feel like going to school. I was sleepy and my body was a little sore. Every time I closed my eyes I had nightmares about car chases and guns firing. The only reason I got on the Internet was so that I could get so sleepy that I had no choice but to fall asleep.

I dragged myself out of bed, put on a pair of jeans and a school T-shirt, and then pulled my hair up in a ponytail. After what happened yesterday, I retrieved the gun out of the shoebox in my closet and slipped it into my backpack. I wasn't going anywhere without it. I would hide it before going into school.

Mom left some money for me on the kitchen counter and I slipped it in my front pocket. I was so used to Ty taking me back and forth to school, that it felt weird walking to the bus stop. I didn't know if it was paranoia or what, but I felt like someone was watching me. Trying to push the paranoia away, I chatted with some of the other kids standing at the bus stop.

"Is that her?" I heard someone yell from a car.

By now the bus was pulling up and blocked their view. So while everyone was loading onto the bus, instead of getting on, I ran through one of the neighbor's yards and to the back. I looked behind me and the bus was still there. This dude walked around and looked on the bus, so I pulled out my cell phone and gun and called Ty. "Baby, come get me. Some people are after me," I blurted in a whisper.

"Where are you?" he asked.

"Right now I'm at the back of the brown house that's right near the bus stop."

"I'm on my way."

I knocked on the neighbor's back door. The elderly woman opened the door. "Dear, what are you doing back there? Shouldn't you be on your way to school?"

"Yes, ma'am. I locked myself out of the house, and my stomach's hurting. I called my mom, and she's on her way home. Can I stay here until she comes?" I lied.

She looked around. "I guess so. I guess it won't be no problem. I was about to head out and run some errands, but I can wait."

"Thank you, Ms. Polly." I looked behind me and felt at ease as I followed her inside. Her house smelled like mothballs. My stomach really was hurting now because the smell was about to make me puke. "Can I use your bathroom?" I asked.

"It's right there," she pointed. "Use some of that Febreeze when you finish."

I dialed Ty's number. "I'm inside the neighbor's house," I said as soon as he answered. "Where are you?"

"I'm driving all the way from Mesquite. Where are the dudes?"

"I don't know."

"Crystal, I need you to look out the window and see if you still see them."

"Okay. I'll call you back," I said.

I flushed the toilet to make it look like I used it. I picked up the bottle of Febreeze and sprayed it.

The doorbell rang as I walked down the hallway. I stopped in mid-step when Ms. Polly answered the door. Evidently, she had a bad habit of not finding out who her guests were before answering her door. I eased back slowly, and I heard the person say, "Ma'am, I was looking for my little sister. She's about yay high."

Ms. Polly said, "Mister, I'm the only one here."

"You mind if I look around?" the guy asked.

After I took a few steps back down the hall, I slipped inside one of her bedrooms. I needed to find a hiding place and fast. I bent down to get under the bed, but there were so many boxes under the bed that I wouldn't be able to fit. Footsteps coming down the hallway sent my heart into overdrive. I ran to the closet and eased it open, hoping it didn't creak. The closet was filled with lots of clothes and shoes and other knickknacks. I went as far back in the closet as I could until I felt the wall. A box fell and hit me upside the head. It hurt. I bit my tongue. I heard Ms. Polly's voice and the man's voice get nearer.

"See, I told you I was home alone," Ms. Polly stated. "I hope you find the girl. There are too many crazy people out there."

"Yes ma'am. There sure is. Well, thank you for letting me look."

"Oh, if it was a child of mine I would be looking for her too."

"I wish there were more concerned citizens like you," he said.

The voices started sounding more distant as they walked back toward the front of the house. I almost peed on myself when the closet door swung open.

"You can come out now, he's gone," Ms. Polly said.

I tripped over clothes as I stumbled out of the closet. "Thank you for not giving me up."

"Next time, tell me the truth," she lectured.

"But I didn't know if you would let me in," I responded.

She removed her hand out of her robe pocket revealing a gun. "Ms. Polly can take care of herself. Now tell me. Why is a pretty girl like you running from a thug like that?"

I shared with her what had transpired in the last twenty-four hours. By then we were seated in the living room. My cell phone vibrated. "It's my boyfriend."

"Are those guys still out there?" Ty asked.

"No. They're gone. Thanks to Ms. Polly," I said when I looked in her direction.

"I'm five minutes away," he responded.

Ms Polly said, "Tell him to come down the back road. Those guys may still be somewhere upfront waiting and watching."

"Thanks. Good looking out. Ty, come down the back road. It'll be like the fifth house when you come from that direction."

Ty hung up with me.

"Be careful," Ms. Polly said as she walked me to the back door.

I hugged her. "Thank you for everything." I shifted my backpack on my shoulder and ran out when I saw Ty's black SUV pull up.

CHAPTER THIRTY-TWO
TY

Crystal jumped inside the SUV once I unlocked the door. I leaned over and hugged her tight. "You don't know how good it is to see you," she said.

I held on to her. After a few seconds, I released her and drove down the alley. I made sure we weren't followed and headed to my hotel. Crystal told me all about her neighbor. "Ms. Polly is packing like Madea." I forced a laugh.

Taking no chances, I parked my car at the back of the hotel. We walked around to where my room was located. I slid the card in. "This is nice," Crystal said once we entered the room.

"It's all right." I threw the card on the table and sat on the bed closest to the door. I patted the bed. "Come. Sit. There's something I need to tell you."

"It's going to have to wait. I need to pee," she blurted out.

I leaned back on the bed with my arms behind my head. As I waited, I closed my eyes and sighed. When she returned, she lay on the bed and placed her head on my chest. I looked down, and her beautiful eyes were staring up at me. I looked away. "I don't know how to say this," I said.

"Ty, just tell me. What is it?" she asked.

I closed my eyes tight. "JC's dead. They killed him."

"No, say it ain't so," Crystal responded. I felt my shirt getting wet with her tears. I wrapped my arms around her, and we held on to each other as we both cried for our friend.

Eventually, our tears stopped and we dozed off. My cell phone rang and woke me up. Crystal shifted on top of me. I gently moved her to the side as I sat up and answered the call.

"I was calling to check on you," Slick said.

"Don't worry about me," I snapped.

"Son, you're my blood. I can't help but worry about you."

"How did your little meeting go?" I asked.

"Son, I'm handling things on this end," he said.

"I can't tell."

"Just give me a little time."

"They came after my girl this morning."

"Are you sure it was them?"

"I'm positive."

My phone clicked. Dang, first my dad called and now Michael. "Hey, I'll call you back," I told Slick right before clicking over.

"How are you?" Michael asked.

"Feel like my whole world is falling apart. Lost my boy last night and almost lost my girl this morning." I told Michael what happened.

"Ty, our Dad needs us."

I laughed. "Please. He got bodyguards and a full compound of weapons. He don't need us."

"Right now, you and I are the only two people he trusts. I can't be there right now, because I'm hot on the block."

"Yeah, I know. JC told me about the bounty on your head."

"I've taught you how to defend yourself. You've taken martial arts and are a great marksman. You may have to put some of those skills to use."

"That's what I was afraid of," I responded.

"Go to him. Let him tell you what needs to be done."

"Michael, you're working with the Feds to take his empire down, so why are you so hell bent on me helping him out?" I asked.

"Trust me when I say that if done right, we can all walk away with our freedom and our lives."

Frustrated, I clenched my fists. "I'm tired. Tired of running. Tired of all of this. Tired of not knowing if somebody is waiting to take me out. I'm tired, man. I'm tired."

"I know, little bro. Just hang on in there a little while longer. So call Slick and do whatever he tells you to do."

"I'll think about it," I responded.

"Do it," Michael repeated.

I looked back at the girl who trusted me with her life. I had to do something, and if that meant going to my daddy to protect Crystal then I would do it. "Fine," I said. "I'll call him and see what I need to do."

"Good. I talked to Mom, and she's going to Louisiana until this thing blows over. Just in case someone has found out about her."

"Well, that's at least some good news," I responded.

"I got to go. Do that and do it now."

I stared at the phone before dialing Slick's number again. He answered before the first ring ended. "Son, I want you to come stay with me. Bring your girl with you." I felt uneasy about it, but really didn't have any other place to go, so I agreed.

"Crystal, wake up," I said as I gently shook her. "We need to get going."

CHAPTER THIRTY-THREE
CRYSTAL

Finding out that JC was dead took its toll on me. First Sade's baby and now JC. I glanced at Ty as he drove to his father's home. I needed to let my parents know where I was so they wouldn't be worried. *But how do I tell them I'm with my boyfriend who has people trying to kill him, and now I'm on my way to his father's house who is a drug kingpin.* Instead, I did what I tried not to do much and lied.

"Turn down the radio," I said to Ty.

He did. I called my mom. "Mom, can I stay over Dena's house? We're going to be rehearsing late, and I can go to school from there." I paused and waited for her response.

"Don't be staying up all night like you did last night. I'll let your dad know."

"Thanks, Mom." I sent Dena a text message to let her know my plans just in case my mom called her house looking for me.

My mouth fell open as we passed by some huge houses. The farther back Ty drove in the area, the bigger the houses got. "Your dad lives here?" I asked.

"Yep," he responded as he pulled up to a guarded gate. Ty rolled down the window.

"Go on in, young blood. Slick's expecting you," the guard said.

The gate opened. I looked from side to side admiring the beauty of the place. "Oh my goodness," I said as we walked up the stairs. I needed to take a picture of those lions because my girls would not believe this.

The front door opened. I followed Ty. A man dressed like the butlers I saw on TV led us down the hall. My mouth remained open in awe. I accidentally bumped into Ty when he stopped.

"Slick, this is Crystal. Crystal, this is my dad."

"I can get used to him calling me that." Slick drew me into a hug.

Slick wasn't what I thought he would be. He looked younger, dressed very well, and smelled really good. He was a good-looking man, and he reminded me of the actor Blair Underwood.

"Have you two eaten?" Slick asked.

"No. I'm not hungry," Ty responded.

"Me neither," I said.

"You two have been through a lot these last twenty-four hours. You need to eat something. I'll have the chef cook you up something."

When Slick left the room, Ty said, "Why did he even ask if he was going to ignore what we said?"

"He's trying to be nice," I whispered.

"Don't let him bully you into doing anything you don't want," Ty said.

"I'm not. Do you think we'll really be safe here?" I asked.

Ty responded, "I hope so."

Slick came back in the room, but he wasn't alone. A woman dressed in a designer dress and her hair looked freshly done walked in behind him. "Crystal, this is Honey. She's going to make sure you have everything you need while you're staying here."

Honey extended her hand. I shook it. She said, "You're about my daughter's size, so I know exactly what size to get you. Let me show you to your room now."

I looked at Ty. He said, "I think it's best that we stay in the same room."

Slick said, "That can be worked out. Let her go see the room. I need to talk to you by yourself for a minute."

I smiled, letting Ty know that it was okay. I followed Honey up the long spiral stairway.

"You're going to love the room. It's right down the hall from where Sam and I sleep," Honey said.

"Who's Sam?" I asked.

"Slick," she responded.

"Oh."

She opened the door and my mouth flew open. The room had a big wooden posted queen-sized bed with a burgundy comforter and several big fluffy pillows. The cherry wood dresser was trimmed in gold. I followed Honey through the room. "Your bathroom is here." She opened the door and allowed me to enter.

"A TV!" I said out loud.

"There's a TV, a telephone, and security screen." Honey showed me how to use each one. "The towels and everything you need are under here." She opened the bottom cabinet drawers. "I'll be right back with some clothes and underwear."

I must have had a strange look on my face. Honey added, "All of the clothes and underwear are brand new. Like I said, you're the same size as my daughter."

"Where's your daughter at now?" I asked.

"She's away at college. She goes to Southern University in Baton Rouge, Louisiana."

"Cool," I responded.

"You're a pretty girl. Be careful. Dating a Davis man comes with a price." Without saying another word, Honey left me alone.

I picked up the remote to the forty-one inch television and started flipping from station to station. Nothing seemed to catch my attention, so I left the TV on an episode of *Gossip Girls*. I threw the remote on the bed. There was a long chair in the corner by the window, so I went and sat down on it. I wasn't prepared for the magnificent view from the window. The room had a beautiful view to the back. I saw a huge pool bigger than my entire house.

"I brought several outfits. You can choose which ones you like. If you like them all, you're welcome to them."

I turned and was amazed that every outfit Honey showed me had tags on them from Saks or Nordstroms. Clothes that I would see some of the rich kids wear at school. I felt like my dreams of wearing designer clothes had come true as Honey left me alone to decide on an outfit. I briefly forgot about all of my problems as I soaked my body in the Jacuzzi and closed my eyes.

CHAPTER THIRTY-FOUR
TY

I was a little uneasy having Crystal out of my sight. The sooner Slick finished talking to me, the quicker she would be right by my side. I took a seat on the sofa and waited for him to finish his phone conversation.

"Son," he said as he sat in his leather recliner. "I'm at a crossroads right now. Everything I built over the years is about to crumble. I've left you and your brother a nice nest egg, so you'll never want for anything."

"You're talking like you plan on dying or something," I said as I sat near the edge of the seat.

"In this game, death is inevitable. I don't want to die and don't plan on dying anytime soon, but just in case, I wanted you to know some things."

"Slick, come on now. We can save this conversation for another day."

He ignored me and kept talking. "Both you and your brother are to get ten million dollars and deeds to several properties. The government nor the law can't touch it, because those funds are legit. My attorney will contact you in the event that something happens to me. I want you to know how much because although the attorney has been with me for years, I don't trust anyone. Right now, your mom is your trustee."

"I'll be seventeen, so I don't need a trustee," I blurted.

"Time flies. I remember holding you and changing your diaper."

I wished I had those memories, but I didn't. I couldn't remember anything about him and that's why growing up, I felt a part of me was missing. "Hard for me to see you changing diapers."

"Changed diapers, warmed up bottles. I was a good dad."

"Why did you bring me into the drug game? You already had one son doing it. Why me too?"

"Son, if I could turn back the hands of time, there's so many things I would do differently. I wanted to leave you boys a legacy. I wanted you two to run this together."

"But that's your dream. I wanted to be a football player." I bit my bottom lip.

"Son, you can be whatever you want. I realize now having you sell drugs was wrong."

"Mom would be so disappointed if she ever found out what you've had me doing."

His eyes had a faraway look. "I would give up the riches and this life if I could go back in time and change things. If I could be the man your mom needed me to be."

Were those tears I was seeing? This was the second time Slick teared up around me. For a hard-core gangster, he sure was sensitive. It made me realize that any resentment that I had, I needed to let it go. His feelings for us were sincere. "I'm supposed to give you this," I said. I stood up and removed the flash drive my brother had given me to show him.

"Your old man isn't that savvy with computers, so I'll need you to pull it up for me," he said. I followed him to the computer on the big mahogany desk. "I just know the basics. Pulling up stuff isn't one of them." I turned on the computer, placed the flash drive in the slot, and then opened up the documents. We exchanged places. He was now seated behind the computer while I stood behind him. The document was filled with information on the men in his organization that were plotting a takeover.

"This is the proof I didn't expect to get," Slick said. He looked up at me. "I brought all of these men into my camp when they were about your age. They were young and hungry. I know what I do isn't exactly right, but I never sold drugs to anyone who didn't want them. I never forced drugs on anyone. Customers tracked me down. I never killed anyone without having a reason to. I left that up to JC's dad."

"You knew JC's dad."

"That was my boy. Called him The Enforcer. He should be out here on these streets with me. There would be no empire without him."

"I don't know how his mom is going to take JC's death. I wish I could be there for her. She let me stay with them."

"You know what. I'm going to make sure she gets everything she needs. Don't worry." Slick stood up. "Turn that off. I got everything on the documents in my memory. Keep the flash drive in a safe place. I'm about to do a major re-org."

The fire in his eyes let me know whoever was on the end of his wrath wouldn't like what was about to happen. I placed the flash drive in my pocket.

"I need to go check on Crystal. She's sacrificed a lot being with me."

"You go check on your girl while I take care of some business," Slick said.

"Yes sir." I walked out of the den and headed up the stairway. I wasn't sure which room she was in, but I would check each room until I found her.

As I walked up the stairway, I heard a voice behind me. "What are you doing here?" Lamb asked.

I turned to face him. His cold, black beady eyes stared up at me. "I'm minding my business," I responded.

Lamb drew his gun on me. "Doughboy, you better show some respect."

"Put that down," Slick said from behind him.

Lamb reluctantly did so. "What is he doing here?" he asked Slick.

"He's a guest of mine, and my guests will not be disrespected."

"He's the one being disrespectful to me," Lamb snapped.

Slick said, "Ty, go ahead and do what you were going to do. Me and Lamb need to have us a little talk."

I smiled. Lamb didn't. Slick put his hand on Lamb's back and led him to the den. I rushed up the stairway in search of Crystal, and I didn't have to look far. She stood in the doorway to one of the rooms.

"I heard your voice, so I came to check it out," she said.

"It's all good. Just looking for you, baby." I walked in her direction.

I hugged her. She smelled like fresh flowers. Crystal moved and I walked inside the room. "This is nice," I said as I looked around.

"Honey gave me some clothes." Crystal showed me the clothes with all of the tags still on them.

"These are nice."

"I know."

"Check out the bathroom." Crystal grabbed my hand and pulled me along.

"A TV. Now this is balling," I said as I pressed buttons on the TV.

"That's the security monitor, so you can see what's going on in the rest of the house."

I used the remote and pressed buttons. The monitor scanned room by room. I paused when I saw my Dad and Lamb. "Hey, I got to use the bathroom. I'll be out in a minute," I said.

Crystal left me alone. Instead of using the bathroom, I tried to see what was going on with Slick and Lamb. My dad was all in Lamb's face. Lamb smirked. My dad went to his desk and was on the phone with his back toward Lamb. On the sneak tip, Lamb put his hand on the gun clipped to his waist. I ran out of the bathroom and then down the stairs. I burst through the den door. Lamb placed the gun back in his side. Dad turned and looked at me with curiosity.

CHAPTER THIRTY-FIVE
CRYSTAL

Ty flew out the room so quick that I wanted to know what was going on, so I ran out behind him. He didn't realize I was right behind him. I waited outside the open door to the den and listened.

"Slick, I need to talk to you about something," Ty said.

"Boy, don't you see two grown men are talking," this other man said. A voice I wasn't familiar with. I tiptoed over and eased my head in to see if I could get a view of the person talking.

"Ugh," I said. He looked like a bug. Mean and ugly were the two best words I could use to describe him.

Slick turned his chair around. "No need for all of that. Ty, I'll be with you in a minute. Lamb and I are through."

Just like that, the little mean and ugly man was dismissed. He didn't seem too happy about it either, because he stormed out headed straight my way. I moved from the pathway of the door. The dude named Lamb stopped and turned around. We were now face to face. He licked his lips. "Haven't seen you here before. I could use a pretty little thing like you in my stable."

Honey stepped in from out of nowhere. "Lamb, I think you better leave this little girl alone. Unless you want the police looking for you for soliciting a minor."

Lamb said a few words under his breath that I couldn't make out and left.

Honey held my shoulders. "You all right? He didn't touch you, did he?"

"No ma'am."

"You sure?" she asked. "Because if he did, I don't care who he is to Slick, I will handle him myself."

"He scared me a little bit, but he didn't touch me."

"Fine. Just be careful. Some of the men that come in here I don't trust them as much as Slick does."

"Honey, is that you?" Slick's voice rang from inside the den.

"Come with me," Honey said.

I followed her into the den. "Your right hand man was harassing Crystal," she said.

Ty rushed over to where I stood. "I'll kill him," he said.

I'd never seen Ty that angry. "I'm fine. He didn't touch me," I assured him.

"What happened?" Slick asked. I told them what happened, leaving out the fact that I was eavesdropping. "He'll be dealt with. I don't stand for my men disrespecting women in my presence," Slick said.

Ty whispered something to Slick and then went back upstairs with me. "Are you sure you okay?" he asked as we now lay across the bed.

"I was concerned about you. You ran out of here like something was after you," I said.

"I saw something on the security monitor that Slick needed to know."

"What?"

"Nothing you need to worry yourself with."

I propped myself up on my elbow. "Ty, what was it? I'm not some fragile little doll, so tell me."

"It looked like Lamb was going to pull a gun out on Slick."

"Are you serious?"

"Yes, and Slick would have been caught off guard because his back was to him. When I burst through the door, Lamb hurried and put his gun back up. Slick had no idea what Lamb was doing. I schooled him on it before I left with you to come back upstairs."

"I thought Lamb was his right hand man. At least that's what Honey told me."

"He is, but not for long. Lamb is the reason why my brother is in hiding. There's a lot of stuff you don't know," Ty confessed.

"I'm listening. I got bullets flying around me. My friend's been killed. My boyfriend can't go anywhere without someone shooting at him. Ty, what in the world is going on?"

"All I can say is that there are men that my dad has trusted for years who are now traitors. They are trying to go behind his back and push my dad out of his own empire."

"Wow. So what's that got to do with Michael though? Did he figure all of this out?" I asked. I'd watched a lot of crime shows on TV.

"Partly, but apparently they learned that if anything happened to Slick that Michael was supposed to take over instead of Lamb. Lamb didn't like learning that, so he's been trying to set my brother up ever since."

The sound of my cell phone ringing interrupted our conversation. I saw a text from my mom. I called her. "I didn't want you to hear it from someone else, but JC's been killed," Mom said. Hearing her say that brought back all of the emotions I felt earlier. Ty rubbed my back as I cried. "You can stay with Dena as long as you need to. Being around your friends right now might help," Mom said.

I laid my head on Ty's chest and cried again.

CHAPTER THIRTY-SIX
TY

If I could erase the pain Crystal was feeling right now I would. We were both grieving over the loss of our friend. Losing JC took the wind out of me. Lamb was responsible for his death, and he would pay, one way or another.

My mind was on ways to seek revenge when I heard a knock at the door. Crystal moved and lay on one of the pillows. I got out of the bed and opened the door. Slick was on the other end. I stepped out into the hallway.

"I don't want to scare you, but things have escalated. I need you to get Crystal, and we need to get out of here. Honey's packing up some stuff now."

"What's going on?" I asked.

"I think Lamb is about to make his move, so we need to get ghost. I have another place that's more secure than this. Nobody, not even Lamb, knows where it's located. Meet me downstairs." Slick handed me a suitcase.

"Baby, get up. We got to go."

Crystal shot up in the bed. "What's going on?"

"Slick wants us to meet him downstairs." I placed the suitcase on the bed and helped Crystal put the stuff Honey gave her in it. I retrieved my duffle bag from under the bed. I grabbed both. "Come on, let's go."

Slick and Honey were waiting for us at the end of the stairway. Slick handed me a set of keys. "You can drive the Benz. It has a full tank and speed if you need it." He whispered in my ear, "I know you strapped, but just in case, there are some guns in the door on both sides."

"Okay."

He handed me a slip of paper. "Just in case we get separated. This is where we're going. The code is on the sheet of paper too. Once you're secure inside, do not open the door for anyone but me."

I don't know why he was telling me this. We were all headed in the same direction. The man who reminded me of Jeffrey from *The Fresh Prince of Bel Air* said, "Master Slick, I will hold down the fort."

"Thanks Bill. I know I can always count on you."

"Always," he responded. Bill looked at me. "Your father is a good man, in spite of the life he's led." I shook my head but didn't say anything as we walked out.

"That's your ride," Slick said, pointing to the black Benz.

I hit the button to unlock the door. As Crystal got in the front seat, I threw our bags in the backseat.

Slick and Honey got into a black Bentley. Slick signaled me to pull up beside him. I did, and then let down the passenger window. "Don't stop for anyone. You hear me?" he said.

My dad was talking to me like I was a child. I heard him the first time. I didn't need him to repeat himself.

The guards opened the gates, and I followed him out of the estate. Soon we were traveling at average speed down the highway. The phone in the car rang. Both Crystal and I looked at it.

"You want me to answer it?" Crystal asked.

"No."

The phone kept ringing. I hit the speaker button.

"Hello," I said.

Lamb laughed like a crazy person on the other end. "This is what happens to traitors."

I heard a loud boom from the other end. Crystal's hand flew to her mouth. "Oh my goodness!" she yelled.

I tried to keep my eyes on the road and on my father, who was steadily moving toward our destination, but after hearing that noise I couldn't concentrate. It startled me. "Lamb!" I called his name several times. No response. Then nothing but a dial tone.

Scared, I pulled out my cell phone and handed it to Crystal. "Scroll through until you come to Bro in the contacts. Call that number."

Crystal's hand shook as she did as I told her. She handed me the phone. I was relieved to hear Michael's voice on the other end. "Things just got more heated. Slick got us leaving his estate and going to another hidden place. Just got a call from Lamb talking about this is what happens to traitors. All I heard is a loud boom like a bomb was set off or something."

Michael responded, "My sources tell me you guys got out just in time. That fool blew up Slick's place."

"Are you serious?" I asked.

"If you noticed I picked up on the first ring. I was about to call you."

I hit the steering wheel. I'd almost lost Slick in traffic. I needed to call him. "Hold the steering wheel, baby," I said to Crystal.

Crystal tried her best to steer from the passenger seat as I did a three-way call with Slick and Michael. "Mike, tell Slick what just happened."

Slick slowed down after hearing the news. I could tell it had gotten to him. "Michael, I need to see you, son. Where are you?"

"Slick, I can't tell you that. Did you do what I told you to do in that message?"

"Not yet," he responded.

I was lost. *What message?* My brother and father were once again keeping me in the dark about things.

"One of us will be in touch when we get situated. Thanks, Michael, for keeping us informed. Ty, we're almost there. Keep up, son," Slick said before hanging up.

"Ty, you all right?" Michael asked.

"This is bull. I can't believe this. I'm roaming here and there without a place to call home. When I think I have a place, then this happens. Man, I don't know how much more of this I can take."

Crystal reached out to try to console me. I pushed her hand away. She didn't reach out again.

"I'll call you when we make it to our destination."

"Be safe," Michael said before I ended the call.

Crystal pouted in the passenger seat. I looked at her and felt guilty for pushing her hand away. "I'm sorry," I said.

"What did you say?" she asked.

I'm pretty sure she heard me the first time, but she wanted to play coy. "I said, I'm sorry."

"Whatever!" she responded.
I deserved that, so I didn't trip on her attitude.

CHAPTER THIRTY-SEVEN
CRYSTAL

I couldn't stay mad at Ty. I knew he had a lot going on, but when he pushed my hand away, I felt like he was rejecting me. I'm right here by his side going through the same thing he's going through. A girl should get some credit for it. A part of me questioned why I didn't listen to Dena and leave Ty alone, but as I sat in the passenger seat and noticed the wrinkles in his forehead from frustration, I knew why I didn't listen to Dena. I loved Ty. I'm really his ride or die chick, and whatever happened, happened. We were in this together.

I yawned. The stress of the day was catching up with me. I leaned back in my seat and looked out the window until we got to our destination. We were north of Dallas on Highway 75 in an area I wasn't familiar with. The last sign I saw said Allen. I'd never been to Allen, Texas before, but I guess there's a first for everything. I shifted in my seat as Ty continued to drive behind his father. Within minutes, we turned off onto a winding road. Like the other place, this place had a gate, but there wasn't a guard. Ty's dad rolled down his window and entered a code. The gate opened and Ty followed him up the driveway.

This house wasn't as big as the other one, but it didn't take away from its beauty. It was still as big as anything I'd ever seen up close and personal. Instead of parking in the driveway, however, we drove into a huge garage.

Ty turned the engine off. I stayed in the car until Ty walked around and opened my door.

"I wanted to park in here just in case we needed a quick getaway," Slick said.

Ty grabbed our bags and we followed Slick and Honey into the house. The door led us into this enormous kitchen. If I ever lived through this and became rich, I wanted a kitchen just like this. Platinum everything. The refrigerator, counters, and stove were all platinum.

"Let me show y'all around. It's best that you both know the layout of the house just in case," Slick said. He looked at Honey. "Dear, make sure everything is fine with their room."

Honey kissed Slick and did as instructed. Ty placed our bags down, and walking hand-in-hand we followed Slick.

Slick hit a switch, and what looked like the den lit up. He went to a bookshelf and removed a book. The bookshelf squeaked and then moved. My mouth flew open in awe. "Come on. What are y'all waiting for?" he said, walking behind the bookshelf into a hidden room.

"What's this?" Ty asked.

"This place is fire proof and leads to an outside tunnel." Slick showed us packaged food, cases of water, weapons and ammunition. It was like a secret hideaway spot. I felt like I was dreaming. I pinched myself and it hurt. This was no dream. I was living the life of a dope dealer's girlfriend, and this life wasn't the one I wanted, but it chose me, so I had to ride it out.

We followed Slick back out into the living room area. He then led us to what would be our bedroom. He opened the closet. Inside the closet were several monitors. "These are in every room so I can see what's going on at all times. Press this button and it will alert me that something is going on." Slick pointed to a big red button on the inside wall of the closet. "There's also a panic button near the bed. He showed us its location.

"Tonight might be the only night we all get some sleep for awhile, so I suggest you both take advantage of it. I'm going to go find Honey and strategize my next move."

Without another word, Slick left Ty and me alone. I sat on the bed. Ty seemed anxious, so he remained standing. He walked over to the window and moved the curtain aside. "Crystal, I'm really sorry about earlier. I'm sorry about everything. I hate I brought you into all of this."

I walked up behind him and placed my arms around his waist. "It is what it is."

"If I would have known all of this drama was going to pop off, I would have just left. JC would still be alive, and

you wouldn't be hiding out with me, fearful for your life."
He squeezed my hands.

"Ty, none of this is your fault. You need to stop blaming yourself. You didn't ask for any of this to happen."

"I know that, but when things started happening with my brother, I should have stayed clear of everybody I love. Now look at things. It's all a huge mess. I'm losing everybody who means anything to me. My mom's had to leave the state so she would be safe."

"Really? I didn't know that," I responded.

"Yes. My brother made sure she went to spend time with family in Shreveport, Louisiana."

"At least you know she's safe. So baby, stop worrying. You got me. Your dad's here. He's not going to let anything happen to you." I tried to assure him.

"He doesn't know who he can trust. And me. I don't trust none of them mo-fos. None of them."

I leaned my head into his back and squeezed him tight. He shifted and we moved toward the bed. "I guess we should get some sleep. I know you're tired," Ty said.

I couldn't hide it. I was exhausted, and I yawned. Ty took off his shirt and then unbuttoned his jeans. I'd watched a lot of movies, but had never seen a boy in person, naked. Ty had the perfect body. I admired his rippled muscular body. I licked my lips, thankful my mom put me on birth control because temptation was staring me straight in the face.

He sat on the bed. I stood and stared. "Are you coming or not?" he asked.

I opened the suitcase to see if there was a nightgown or pajamas or something I could put on to hide my body. Nothing. Ty handed me one of his T-shirts from his bag. "You can wear this."

I took it. "Thanks." I turned my back to him and undressed. Then I put his T-shirt on. It fit me like a nightshirt. I slipped under the covers beside him.

"You're so beautiful," Ty said as he looked into my eyes.

"Thanks." I blushed.

He wiped the hair from my forehead. "I mean it. You're beautiful from the inside out. I'm the luckiest boy in Texas."

Without another word, Ty bent down and started kissing me. I kicked the covers off me because it was getting hot. His hands roamed all over my body. I started feeling things I had never felt before. A moaned escaped my lips, but visions of the pregnant girls from the clinic popped in my head. I tried to block them out. No such luck. Ty used one hand to open my thighs, but I used my hand to block him. I couldn't do it. As much as my body was saying one thing, the voice of reason stepped in and stopped me from going further.

"I love you, Ty, but I'm just not ready."

"Baby, I understand." Ty kissed me on the forehead and held me.

CHAPTER THIRTY-EIGHT
TY

Crystal got a brother wanting her so bad, but I promised to respect her wishes. So all I could do was hold her tight and try to think of something else, but it was hard when she smelled like fresh peaches. I wrapped my arms around her waist as our heartbeats and breathing fell in sync with each other. I zoned out, and before I realized it, I had slipped off into sleep. In my dream, Crystal and I were dancing and having a good time. I kept hearing someone call my name. The room began to shake. I held on to Crystal tighter. Then my eyes flew open.

"Ty, I hear something," Crystal whispered as she shook me.

Awake and fully alert, I was no longer dreaming. I reached on the side of the bed, grabbed my weapon, and pointed to the closet. Crystal went to the closet. I tiptoed to the door and hit the lock button. Once it was securely locked, I went to the closet to look at the monitors.

Crystal's hand was over her mouth. What was she looking at? She pointed at the upper right of the screen.

Several masked men were going from room to room. I hit the panic button to alert my dad just in case he didn't hear. "Put something on, because we might have to jet," I told Crystal.

I watched the monitors as we dressed in the closet. My shoes were by the bed. I wouldn't worry about shoes right now. One of the masked men stopped at our door and turned the knob, but it wouldn't budge. He motioned one of the other masked men to come over. The guy took out a slim gadget that looked similar to a small screwdriver and inserted it. He moved the knob until the lock became loose. I stepped in front of Crystal. She trembled. I stooped down and pulled out a gun and handed it to her. "When that closet door opens, shoot and don't stop shooting until you hear me say stop," I whispered.

Crystal nodded. I held my breath as I saw the guys search under the bed and the bathroom. "Get on the floor. Shoot from in between my legs," I directed Crystal. She eased herself down on the carpeted floor. I heard the doorknob move.

"Get ready," I whispered.

The door swung open, and I opened fire and so did Crystal. We caught both assailants off guard because neither got a chance to get a shot off before falling to the floor. Not sure of where the other assailants were at this point, but I had to get Crystal out of there. I'm sure they heard the gunshots and would be headed this way. I rushed past the downed assailants. Crystal whimpered as she followed suit. I grabbed the car keys and my bag. Then I stuck my head in the hallway to see if anyone was coming. I didn't see anyone. "Come on," I mouthed.

Crystal held her gun at her side as we tiptoed down the hallway. I saw the shadow of someone coming. "Fall back." I ended up pushing Crystal into another room and gently closed the door. We were trapped. I hoped that Slick and Honey were okay, but my first and top priority was right here next to me. I felt her body trembling. I had to think of something and think of something quick.

"Hey, this door opens," Crystal said.

I looked behind her. The door led to some stairs. Perfect. It was dark. I waited a few minutes until my eyes adjusted to the darkness. Crystal shut the door, turned, and held on to the loop of my jeans as I eased down the stairs. I almost screamed when I bumped into a body.

"Shh," Slick said. Beside him was Honey. Even in the darkness, I could see that she was bleeding.

"You warned me just in time. Before I could get us out of harm's way, one of them clipped Honey."

"Stop all of this talking and get us the hell out of here," Honey said, holding on to her thigh.

"We're not going anywhere," Slick said. "We're outnumbered. It's six of them and two of us."

"Let's say its four now. We put two down."

"Okay, then four. We need to get those four and secure these premises. It seems my entire security details have been compromised," Slick said, sounding frustrated.

"No time for small talk. Slick, do something," Honey said.

Slick asked, "What do you have in the bag?" He pointed to the flashlight he had on my bag.

I pulled out several weapons. He took one and handed Honey one. "I got some more clips zipped up on the side."

"You girls stay here. Shoot anything that moves," Slick said. "Come on, son. We're not going to sit here and be sitting ducks."

I chose not to look at Crystal because I didn't want to see the fear in her eyes. I followed Slick back up the stairs. "Be prepared to shoot," he said.

He didn't have to tell me twice. My life and Crystal's depended on it.

CHAPTER THIRTY-NINE
CRYSTAL

"Hold me up, dear," Honey said.

She wrapped her arm around me as I helped her down the stairs. We got to the bottom and she sat down. I stood facing the door, just in case someone came through it.

"You're holding that gun like you know what to do with it," Honey said.

"I'm trying not to think about it."

"You remind me of my daughter. Feminine but strong when she needs to be," Honey said as she winced in pain.

"I didn't want to worry Ty, but I'm scared. I'm really scared."

"Everything is going to work out."

We both turned in the direction of the noise and heard several shots coming from upstairs. Honey tried to encourage me, but I could tell she was just as worried. "Help me up. We need to make sure they are okay," she said.

"But, Slick told us to stay down here."

"We're not going back up the stairs. Just do what I tell you," she said.

I allowed Honey to lead the way. We ended up in the garage. "Let go!" she said, steadying herself on her injured leg and clenching her teeth. "It hurts, but I can do this." She took a step and each step looked easier. "Come on. Keep your gun pointed."

Honey snuck in through the kitchen door. As I followed her, I heard a crash from behind me. Immediately, I turned and shot without looking. I didn't realize I hit anyone until I spotted a guy on the floor holding on to his chest, cursing and calling me all sorts of names.

"I can't believe you shot me!" the man said over and over. The gun flew from his hands to the other side of the kitchen.

"Get the gun!" Honey directed.

I picked up the gun and placed it on the counter.

Honey pointed her gun at the guy. "How many more of you is there?" she asked.

"I'm not telling you nothing," he said, holding on to his bleeding chest. I couldn't believe I'd actually shot two guys.

"I thought I told y'all to stay put," Slick said as he entered the kitchen. Ty walked in right behind him.

Honey said, "Looks like it's this guy's lucky day."

Slick looked down. "Pork, wasn't I good to you?"

Pork didn't respond. Slick kicked him in the arm. "Answer me. Wasn't I good to you?"

"Uh-uh-uh," he stuttered.

"What is Lamb promising you that you would betray me?" Slick asked. "Help his ass up," he said to Ty.

Ty moved quickly and picked the guy up. The man cried out in pain. Blood dripped on the floor. Slick laughed.

"You let a woman almost take you out. I don't need you in my camp anyway."

"Man, what are you going to do?" Pork asked.

"Baby, what do you think I should do?" Slick looked at Honey.

"He means nothing to me." Honey looked away.

"Again. What is Lamb promising you?"

"He said I would be his right hand man. All I had to do is take you out."

Slick laughed. "And you thought it would be easy. Come on, man. You should know me better than that. Everything Lamb knows, I taught him. The student is never better than the teacher."

Honey said, "School him, baby."

"Don't kill me. I can tell you everything," Pork begged.

"I know all I need to know. Two of the people I trusted are traitors. I don't need to know anything else."

I watched Slick point the gun at Pork's head.

Ty said, "Dad, don't. Not in front of Crystal."

Slick looked at Ty and then back at Pork. "This is your lucky day." Slick dropped his arm with the gun and placed it on the counter.

Pork started spewing out things. "Lamb is expecting me to call him to let him know you've been eliminated. If I don't call him, he's only going to send out another set of men to complete the job."

Slick reached in Pork's pocket and located his cell phone. He sat down at the kitchen table on the opposite side of Pork. "I suggest you make the call. Tell him you put two in the dome."

"He's going to want to see proof," Pork said.

"Tell him you'll bring him the body. Do it, or nothing my son or anyone else says will stop me from shooting you directly between your eyes."

I held my breath to see what would happen next.

CHAPTER FORTY
TY

I wrapped my arm around Crystal and led her out of the kitchen. "What happened back there?" I asked.

"I heard a noise and turned around and shot like you told me," Crystal responded.

"Remind me not to mess with you, Ms. Sharp Shooter."

We both chuckled, although both of us were stressed out.

"Did y'all get the other guys?" she asked.

"We need a cleanup crew for the dead bodies," I responded.

"So those guys we shot . . . are they really dead?" Crystal asked.

"I'm afraid so."

Crystal started crying. I wrapped my arm around her, hoping to provide some type of comfort.

"Baby, it was either them or us. We only did what we had to do."

"I know, but dead . . . I can't believe I'm responsible for taking someone else's life."

I held Crystal's hand and turned her so we were facing one another. "Look at me."

She looked up at me. I said, "If we wouldn't have shot them, they were going to kill us. We had no choice. Besides, it could have been either one of our bullets. If it'll make you feel better, we can say it was bullets from my gun that killed him."

Slick came out in the hallway. "Son, I need you to watch Pork. Don't let him out of your sight. I got some things to take care of. I need to get ready to confront Lamb."

"Crystal, can you drive?" Slick asked.

"Yes," she responded.

"Good. I will need you to drive Honey to a friend's house. He's a doctor, and he'll get her all fixed up."

"I don't think we should separate," I said.

"Son, there's no other way."

Crystal looked at me. I tried to assure her things would be okay. I hadn't asked, but while I was seated watching Pork, Crystal returned to the kitchen with my shoes. She had put hers on and was waiting for Honey to come back in the kitchen.

"Baby, be careful. You got your phone?" I asked.

She patted her pockets. By now she had my T-shirt tucked in her jeans. Under normal circumstances, I would be admiring her curves. Pork moaned.

"I need to lay down," Pork said.

"I'm not trying to make you comfortable."

Pork leaned on the table. Honey popped him upside the head when she walked by him. "I ought to shoot you myself for dripping blood all on my kitchen floor and table." Honey walked near Crystal. "Come on, baby. Let's get out of here."

Crystal and I hugged. I watched them leave through the kitchen door. "Get up," Slick said as he came back in the room. Slick had changed into all black. He was carrying several big duffle bags.

"Son, there's a bag outside the den door. I need you to go get it." Slick handed me some black jeans and a black T-shirt with a black skullcap. "Put these on while I bandage him up so he can stop bleeding on everything."

I quickly changed and threw my clothes on the chair. Then I went to the den. The huge black bag was very long. I bent to pick it up, but strained a little because it was heavy. I carried it into the kitchen.

"What's in this thing? A missile?" I asked.

"You got it," Slick responded.

I made sure I was careful with it. I held on to the bag and pushed Pork toward the door. Once outside, I opened the front door to the SUV and put him in the passenger side.

"You're going to drive," Slick said, jumping into the backseat.

I got behind the wheel. "Where to?" I asked.

Pork moaned in pain.

Slick said, "We're going to another one of my spots that's not so heavily guarded. Keep that baseball hat tilted on your head when you drive up. And you." Slick was now talking to Pork. "You better not say anything out of line."

"I promise you, boss."

Slick gave me directions as I drove. It didn't take long to get to our destination. As tired as I'd been, my adrenaline had me pumped up.

We pulled up to the front door. One of the men who my father used to trust came to the passenger side.

Pork said, "Man, where Lamb at?"

"Waiting for you to bring him Slick's dead body," the man responded.

"He in the back. My boy here will help you take the body in," Pork responded.

That was my cue to get out and open the passenger door. I walked to the other side of the SUV, pretending to be pulling Slick. When the dude bent his head over and was partially in the backseat, Slick got him in a choke hold. I looked around to make sure no one saw us. They didn't, so I pushed the dude farther in. One down, and no telling how many more to go.

Slick exited the back of the car. We were dressed just like the men we killed back at Slick's place. All black with black skullcaps.

"Get out!" Slick said to Pork.

Pork remained seated. Slick jerked him out. Pork lost his balance, and if I hadn't stepped in and caught him, he would have hit the ground.

"Come on," Slick said.

I helped Pork walk up on the porch and into the house. Loud music could be heard. Some of the dudes we ran into looked like they were either high or drunk or both. Slick shook his head in disgust as he noticed some of his foot soldiers obviously celebrating the fact that he was supposedly dead.

I kept my hand on my Glock, never knowing when someone would recognize me and try to do me harm. It amazed me that these fools were so busy celebrating, that they didn't realize the man walking in with Pork was not dead but the one and only Slick.

CHAPTER FORTY-ONE
CRYSTAL

Honey gave me directions to the doctor's house. When we arrived, he didn't seem surprised to see us. He helped Honey out of the car. I sat in the background as he took her to his home based operating room.

I made myself busy by flipping stations on the television. My mind wasn't on any of the shows, instead it was on Ty. I wondered if this would be our last time seeing each other.

The doctor came back in where I was. "The bullet was stuck in her leg, but I was able to get it out. Honey is a tough chick. Give her a few minutes and she'll be ready to go."

I felt relieved for the first time. Although I'd just met Honey, I'd grown attached to her and didn't want anything to happen to her.

She limped in the room dressed in a pair of shorts and T-shirt, but her face wasn't grimacing in pain like before.

"The good doctor has given me some feel good medicine for the pain. In a couple of days, I'll be like new. "

"I'm just glad you're all right," I said.

"Me too. Now come on because we need to go help out our men."

"But isn't it unsafe?" I asked.

"Being with a Davis man period is unsafe. If you're going to be with Slick's son, you must get used to it."

Her words sent a chill up and down my spine. I loved Ty and would do anything for him, but I questioned whether I could get used to it.

My phone vibrated. I hoped it was Ty calling me, but it was Dena. I hit the reject button as Honey and I walked to the car.

"You did such a good job driving us over here. I'm going to let you drive us to Slick's other place."

I reluctantly got behind the wheel and followed Honey's instructions. "Hey, stop here. We're going to walk the rest of the way," Honey said, about thirty minutes later.

"Are you sure? What about your leg?"

"I'll be okay. Come on." I turned off the engine and got out to follow Honey. She stopped.

"On second thought, my gut is telling me that we might need to stay in the car. Get back in and drive close to the front."

Confused by her change of heart, I was too scared not to follow her instructions. I pulled the car up to the front of the house. I recognized the SUV that Ty and Slick had left in earlier.

"They're in there. I can't go in because they all recognize me. But you're a new face. Take this." Honey handed me a weapon. I already know you know how to use it. I'm going to slip behind the driver's seat. Bring our men out so we can get the hell up out of here."

I had no idea what I was doing, but like a fool I got out of the car with the gun in my pocket. Music was heard as soon as I walked in the door. The guys were gawking at me, but no one said anything as I made my way inside in search of Ty.

Some dude blocked my entrance. "The party is in the back. We got everything you need back there, pretty lady."

"I'm good. I was looking for the bathroom."

"The bathroom is down the hall," he replied as he licked his lips.

Thanks." I walked in that direction, but turned to see if he was looking at me. He'd gone on about his business.

I tiptoed down the hall, and I heard a boom. That had to be where Ty was. Instead of running in the opposite direction of the sound, I ran toward it and almost tripped over a dead body.

Ty, Slick, and that Pork fellow were walking to another room. I followed them without being noticed. They knocked on the door and someone let them in. The door didn't close all of the way, so I was able to see what was going on.

So far, it looked like they didn't realize Slick was Slick. They had to be some dumb ones, but I was only fifteen so what did I know. I could see Lamb's expression when he looked up and noticed Slick walking in with Pork. His delay of reacting cost him, because Slick moved so fast with his Glock and shot one strait in the skull. Lamb fell down dead. My hand flew to my mouth.

The other men in the room started shooting. Ty pushed Pork's body out front and shielded himself. I had to do something, but fear had me frozen in place. With the music being loud, people on the other side of the house didn't hear the shots and kept partying like nothing was going on.

Mesmerized as I watched Slick and Ty kill the men in the room. "Come on!" I heard Slick say." They rushed out of the door and bumped right into me.

"What are you doing here?" Ty asked.

"No time. Come on, we need to get out of here," Slick said.

"Honey's waiting in the car out front," I said.

Ty pulled me along as we rushed out. Someone yelled behind us because apparently, they saw the bloodbath Slick and Ty left. There was a lot of confusion going on as gunshots rang out.

"Run to the car!" Ty yelled. He didn't have to tell me twice. I headed straight for the front door.

"What the hell?" one of Lamb's cronies yelled and pulled out his gun.

I ducked and Ty shot him. We all slipped out the front door. I jumped in the car with Honey.

Ty and Slick grabbed some bags out of the SUV and jumped in the backseat. Slick said, "Gun it!"

Honey sped off as bullets flew around us. I bent down as far in my seat as I could. I glanced outside and saw men getting in cars. We were being chased.

Slick said, "Slow it down a minute."

"But we got those fools after us," Honey said.

"Just do what I said!" Slick yelled.

Honey slowed down. Slick removed this long metal device from the black bag. He rolled the back window down and stuck it outside. He hit a button. The next thing I heard was a loud boom. I turned and saw the car behind us explode, and the car that was near it ran straight into the fire and debris.

If you would have told me a few weeks ago I would be involved in some stuff like this, I would have looked at you like you were crazy. I went from a dull, normal life to life on the far edge.

CHAPTER FORTY-TWO
TY

Sweat poured down my face. Breathing heavily, I fell back on the seat. Things had spiraled out of control. Up until this week, I'd never killed a man. This week I'd lost count of how many I've had to kill to protect the people I love. I glanced at the man in the seat next to me. My emotions were all over the place, but I knew that I would do anything to protect the man who fertilized my seed. When faced with death, it would definitely bond you to people.

Honey continued to drive fast. We heard sirens. Honey let out a few obscenities. "I don't have my license," she yelled.

We thought the police were going to pull us over, but instead when Honey slowed down, they ended up passing her.

Honey drove us back to the house. When we got there, the bodies that were there had been removed. I asked, "What happened here?"

Slick responded, "Your brother took care of this."

I really needed to talk to Michael. I pulled out my cell and dialed his number but didn't get an answer.

When I turned around Crystal was right there. I could barely move. "Baby, I'm not going anywhere. I'm right here," I said, attempting to reassure her.

Crystal wouldn't let me out of her sight, and I wouldn't let her out of mine. We went to another one of the bedrooms because neither one of us felt comfortable in the old room after having to kill those two guys. There wasn't a bathroom in it, so we took turns using the bathroom down the hall.

My mind and body were exhausted. I fell asleep, but instead of falling into a deep slumber, I slept lightly. The slightest sound woke me up. I didn't want anyone else to be sneaking up on us.

The next morning I woke up to the aroma of food. Once Crystal and I dressed, we headed to the kitchen. Honey had gotten up early and cooked a huge Texas style breakfast filled with bacon, eggs, grits, and biscuits.

"Help me take this to the dining room," Honey directed us.

I almost dropped the tray of food I was holding when I saw Michael seated at the table next to my daddy.

"Michael!" I excitedly said as I put the platter of food on the table.

He stood up and gave me a brotherly hug. I took a seat next to him.

Slick said, "We have a lot to discuss, but for now, I want to enjoy breakfast with my two sons."

Not much was said over breakfast. We were all hungry because the platters of food were empty in a short amount of time.

"I'll help you with the dishes," Crystal said when Honey got up.

"Thanks, dear. Men, we'll leave y'all to talk."

"Follow me," Slick said, easing from behind the table.

We followed him into the living room. He handed Michael a cigar and lit it. He looked at me. "You're still not old enough to indulge in this pleasure."

I took a seat on the couch.

"The reason why I came out of hiding is there's something I need to tell you," Michael said.

"Son, you don't need to hide anymore. The problem has been eliminated. The men who were following Lamb are scrambling and wondering what's going to happen next. They shifted their allegiance to him and don't know what I'm going to do next."

"That's the thing, Slick. Lamb is just part of the problem."

"What do you mean, son?" Slick asked.

Slick sat down. Michael had both of our attention. "The Feds busted me, and I had to do something, or I was facing fifty years in jail."

"Anytime the Feds are involved it can't be good. So what are you telling me, son? Are you telling me you're a rat?"

Michael looked away as if he was ashamed. "I never gave them your name. And that's even before I knew you were my father."

"So what did you do?" Slick puffed on the cigar several times.

"I gave them enough information to take down some of your operations. They are mainly looking for your supplier, and you were going to be icing, but they weren't concerned about getting you."

"Sure they aren't. Don't you know they know everything there is to know about you? I bet you someone knows you're here talking to me now," Slick said.

"You're probably right. When Jay turned on me, I knew I had to do something. I found out he was working with Lamb. Lamb was going to feed you to the Feds, but if that didn't work he was going to have someone take you out."

"He was too big of a coward to do it himself," I said.

"Well, he's dead now," Slick said.

"That's a good thing, because I sort of made it look like Lamb was the mastermind behind the whole operation," Michael said.

"Oh really." Slick leaned back in his chair and crossed his leg.

"That's why I'm here. I think it's best that you get all of your available legal assets and relocate as soon as possible. I don't know when, but the Feds are going to be raiding anything that's associated with the business."

"Fortunately for me, I was smart enough not to put anything in my name." Slick laughed. "Several things are in Lamb's legal name. Guess he was going to pay for betraying me one way or another."

"I know. That's the list the Feds will get." Michael looked at me. "Do you have that flash drive I gave you? I need it back."

"Yes, I got it." I removed the necklace from outside of my shirt, removed the flash drive from it, and handed it to Michael.

Michael took it and put it in his shirt pocket. "Pops, you got twenty-four hours to get out of town before I turn this in." Michael patted his pocket.

"You better be glad you're my blood, son, or I would have to kill you."

"I'm sorry, but I did what I thought I needed to do."

"Yes, to save your own skin. All you had to do is come to me, and I would have gotten you the best attorneys that money could buy."

"I couldn't take that chance. I wanted my life, but Lord knows I've been more fearful of my life since I agreed to work with them."

"So that's one thing Lamb wasn't lying about. You were trying to sell me up the river." Slick's face tensed up.

"Pops, no. All the evidence I have points at Lamb, not at you."

"I guess I should feel lucky that it does." Slick stood, went to the bar, and poured him a drink. He held out another glass. "You want some?"

Michael declined. I remained quiet. I didn't know what Slick's next move would be, and if I had to, I would take out my own father to protect my brother. Michael had been my protector when Slick wasn't around, so Michael was who I pledged my allegiance to.

Slick took a couple more swigs of his drink before placing the glass on the bar. "Well, I guess I should be grateful and thank you for giving me a head start." Slick held out his hands wide. "I'm going to have to leave all of this behind. Everything I've built over the last fifteen years."

"You can always come back to Dallas when things cool down," Michael said.

Slick shook his head. "No. I always knew this day would come. Honestly though, I thought I would be leaving here in a body bag. I guess I should thank you for making me take an early retirement where I walk away with my life."

Michael stood up. "Even before I knew you were my dad, I felt a connection with you. I'm sorry."

Slick patted Michael on the back. "No need to be sorry. As I stand here and think about it. I may have done the same thing. Then again, I don't know. I don't fault you for it. You did what you needed to do for you and Ty." Slick looked at me. I didn't want to get all emotional, so I looked away. "I told Ty that if anything happened to me, you both were set up nicely with ten million dollars. With me leaving, that still stands. I signed the papers, so in about two weeks you two will have access to it. I did that the moment I realized there were some traitors amongst me."

My mouth flew open. In a few weeks I would be seventeen and a millionaire. I couldn't wait to share the news with Crystal.

FORTY-THREE
CRYSTAL

Ty walked in the bedroom all excited. I sat up in bed, hoping he had some good news for me.

"Guess what?" he asked. "My dad's giving me ten million dollars for my birthday."

I would be lucky to get a party. Ty was getting millions of dollars. Somebody pinch me. This was surreal. "Wow!" was all I managed to say.

"The only thing is, he's going to have to leave town, and I may not ever see him again after today."

"Why is that? Even if he moves, you can always visit," I said as I attempted to comfort him.

"No. When he leaves, for now it'll be best that we don't have any communication."

"Oh." I don't know how I would feel if I couldn't talk to my dad. Just these hours away from my parents had me missing them.

"It's cool. It's not like I'm used to him being around anyway. I just wished that we had a little more time to get to know each other."

"You have the rest of the day."

Ty ignored me. He said, "Turn that up."

"What?" I asked.

He picked up the remote near me and turned up the volume on the television. The news showed several body bags being taken out of the house where we were last night. The reporter said, "Several men were shot and killed. Witnesses said they were not able to identify the shooter. We do know that there were at least two shooters from eye-witnesses."

We sat and watched as the body bags were placed in the back of the ambulance.

"Seems like nobody's talking. I'm sure they know exactly who did it," Ty said.

"Maybe they don't," I said.

"Oh, believe me they do. Anybody who was left alive knows it was Slick who killed Lamb, Pork, and the rest of those guys. They are running scared. Not sure of what Slick's next move is going to be."

"I hate that so many people have lost their lives," I said, curling my body up into a ball.

Ty wrapped his arm around me. "Me too, but like I said before, it was either them or us. And I'd kill a hundred mo-fos before I let one take out my girl."

"So what's next? When your dad leaves what are you going to do? Where are you going to stay?" My mind was filled with a load of questions.

"Him and Michael insist I get back into school. I'm trying to tell them the school year is over. I guess I'll enroll in summer school so I can pass to the next grade, or else you and I will be in the eleventh grade together next year."

"That's not so bad," I said, smiling for the first time.

"For you, no; but for me, I'm too smart to flunk."

"I'm just glad you're deciding to hang around," I said.

"Crystal, we've been through too much. There's no way in the world I would leave you now. Nothing, and I do mean nothing can separate us."

At that moment in time, Ty and I were the only two people in my world that mattered. I couldn't care less what either one of my best friends said. They didn't know what we'd been through. I'd seen the fire in Ty's eyes when death stared us both in the face. He was determined to protect me or die trying. If I had any doubts about his feelings for me before, I didn't have any now. I knew he loved me and I loved him too.

"Knock. Knock," Honey said from the doorway.

We both sat up.

"Your brother is about to leave and wanted to see you," Honey said to Ty.

"Come on." Ty extended his hand to help me off the bed.

We walked down the hallway behind Honey.

Michael stood near the front door. "Lil Bro, I'm about to be underground for a few weeks. Next time I talk to you, you'll be seventeen."

"It's going to be hard not talking to you," Ty said.

"I know. All you need to do is what we talked about. Lay low and just concentrate on school. I want to see you back on that football field."

Slick added, "Because you're the next Emmitt. I've been to some of your games."

Ty looked at Slick. "Really?"

"Yes. Although I wasn't a part of your lives, I did keep up with what you were doing."

Ty shrugged his shoulders. "I guess."

Michael looked at his watch. "My time here is up. I got to move on to my next destination."

Michael and Ty hugged. I wiped the tears that threatened to fall.

"Crystal, thanks for holding my brother down." I smiled.

Without another word, Michael left.

Slick handed Ty some papers. "This is the deed to a condo. It's all yours."

Ty glanced at the papers. "It has my mom's name on it."

"I know. She wouldn't take it, and I never had the heart to sell it. So now it's yours if you want it. I paid the realtor to rent it out. The last tenants moved out a few months ago. All you'll need to do is buy some furniture. There's some old furniture there, but I'm sure you'll want to change it out. With all the money I left you, I'm sure that won't be a problem."

"Thanks, Dad." Ty hugged Slick.

Slick held on to Ty. I couldn't hold back the floodgates of tears. I watched as Ty and Slick took their relationship to another emotional level. For a hardcore gangster, Slick seemed to have a sensitive side. I no longer looked at him as being the monster that people in the neighborhood described him as. I'm sure very few people were privileged enough to see this vulnerable side to the man I used to call a 'street giant'.

Honey cleared her throat, breaking up the sentimental moment. "Baby, we got to get moving so we can make that flight."

"Where are y'all going?" I asked Honey.

She looked at me with pity in her eyes. "Baby girl, I wish I could tell you. I know we just met, but I love you as if you were my own daughter. Promise me that you will keep him"—she pointed to Ty—"out of trouble."

"I'll try," I responded.

Ty placed his arm around me. "I've had enough of the thug life. She's not going to have to do too much because all I plan to do is go to school and work out."

Slick said, "That's my boy."

We all smiled, enjoying the quiet moment.

FORTY-FOUR
TY

"Will you spend the night with me at my new place?" I asked Crystal as we packed up the little of our belongings.

"Sure. My mom's not expecting me home anytime soon," Crystal responded.

"Good, because I need you tonight."

I grabbed our bags and took them to the front door. Slick had several designer bags at the front door. "Ladies, you wait right here while we go pack the cars."

"My car was at your place. I'm sure it's all blown up," I said.

"The Benz is yours," Slick said.

"Are you serious? Aw man. I can't believe it."

"Believe it. It's yours." I took our bags and placed them in the trunk of the Benz.

Honey and Crystal were walking out the door. They stood at the door and hugged. Crystal walked over and Slick embraced her. "If my son gets out of line, you know what to do."

Crystal chuckled. She got in on the passenger side.

Slick looked at me. "Well, son, this is it. I hate we're just now getting to know each other, but know this—that I love you no matter what happens in this life. I always have." Slick pulled me into a father and son embrace again.

"I love you too, Dad," I said. He patted me on the back. This time Slick didn't care if I saw the tears. He allowed them to freely flow down his cheeks.

"Your old man is getting soft in his old age."

"You still got it, Pops."

"Pops. Dad. A man can get used to being called either one of those things." He laughed away the tears. "This is hard. I can leave behind the property, the money, but leaving you behind for a second time . . . It's hard." Slick held his head down and moved it from side to side.

"Pops, you heard what Michael said. If you don't get out of town, you could be doing some serious time. I would rather know you're safe somewhere else than locked up in a jail cell."

"I know. I will be in touch when I can. Not directly, but you'll know it's me," Slick said.

Honey said, "Baby, it's time."

"You better get going," I said.

"Take care, son," Slick said as he walked to his car.

"You too, Dad." I walked to get in my new car.

Neither one of us wanted to be the first to pull away. Slick put his arm out the window and motioned for me to go. I started up the car and drove away. I blew the horn in passing and he blew his.

"Where do you think they are going?" Crystal asked.

"Some place where there's no extradition back to the U.S. is all I know," I responded. "He wouldn't tell me where either."

"Oh." Crystal looked away and out of the window.

I reached over the seat and held her hand. I drove to what would become my new home. The condo was near a man-made lake and in a quiet neighborhood with different races of people. I was glad of that so that way I wouldn't stand out.

"This is home," I said as I flipped on the lights as we entered the living room.

"Nice. Very nice," Crystal responded.

"It sure is." I went from room to room inspecting it.

The furniture here was nice. I didn't think I needed to buy any new furniture. The bedroom was humongous. Not as big as the one at my dad's houses, but bigger than anything I'd been accustomed to. The only thing new I would buy would be a new bedroom suite. But for now, it would do until Crystal and I could go shopping.

I called and ordered pizza. Crystal and I had a nice romantic pizza dinner. We filled our cups with Sprite and toasted. "To sharing a new life with the love of my life," I said.

The next day I hired some movers to go by my old place. I drove there to let them know which things I was taking. I made Crystal stay in the car. Satisfied that the movers had packed all the things I wanted or needed, they followed me to my new place. The whole process took about five hours and that included traffic.

Crystal and I curled up on the couch, and I turned on the local news. "There was a bad wreck on Northwest Highway that left several people dead. The victims have finally been identified." I listened as my dad and Honey's name were read. "No, it can't be," I yelled out.

Crystal tried to comfort me by wrapping her arms around, but I was too upset to sit still. I paced the floor back and forth. It took all of these years to find him and now this. Just when my life was getting on track.

Crystal called my name several times. "It's your brother. You might want to answer it." She handed me my phone. I clicked the button.

"Man, have you heard? Can you believe it?" I blurted.

Michael said, "Calm down."

"I can't. Man, I'm losing it over here."

"That's why I'm calling you. All is well."

"No it isn't," I said.

"Yes, it is. Listen to me, Ty. All is well."

It finally dawned on me what he meant. "So they aren't?" I didn't complete my statement.

"No. Will be in touch."

Before saying another word, Michael disconnected the call.

I yelled out, "Thank God!"

"What's going on?"

I sat down beside Crystal. "They are alive."

"Baby, we just saw they were killed in the car crash."

"No, you don't understand. Michael called me to let me know they are alive."

Crystal hugged me. We rocked back and forth as I calmed my nerves. Slick was alive, and regardless if I ever saw him again; knowing he was alive meant there was always a possibility that we could build a father-son relationship. If he was dead, then that would be a wrap. I wasn't ready to close the door on Slick.

FORTY-FIVE
CRYSTAL

Ty and I had been so wrapped up in our little world of drama that we weren't prepared when JC's mom called to give him funeral details. She had him listed as a pallbearer.

"Crystal, I don't know if I can do it. I don't know if I'll be able to hold the casket of my best friend." Ty placed his head on my shoulder, and I allowed him to release his pain.

"You have to. Do it for his mom," I said.

Ty reluctantly agreed to do so.

When I went back home, it seemed strange to be in the bed by myself. Ty and I stayed on the phone for hours. We knew the next day would be a difficult one.

On Saturday morning, Ty stopped by to pick me up. We were both dressed in black. I said good-bye to my family as we left for Second Street Missionary Baptist Church on the south side of Dallas.

I sat on the second row next to Ty. My parents and little sister were seated several rows behind me. The funeral was short but long at the same time. I wanted it to be over.

Ty never let go of my hand. The funeral was coming to a close. Ty would need to do his duties as pallbearer. He squeezed my hand tight.

I whispered, "You can do it."

He placed his shades over his red, watery eyes. The pallbearers walked JC's blue casket down the middle aisle. We all stood up and followed the processional. I stopped when I got to my parents' pew, so they could come out with me. My mom held on to my hand.

"Baby, he's in a better place. His mom told me he was baptized, so be assured he's with our heavenly Father."

"I know, Mama," I said in between sniffles.

When I heard JC's mama yell, "My baby!" It almost brought me to my knees. Mom had to hold me up. Cries could be heard as we walked out the front of the church.

My dad asked, "Are you going to ride with us or Ty?"

"Ty," I responded.

"Okay. Everybody's coming to the house, so we expect y'all to show up," he said.

"Yes, sir."

I decided not to follow Ty to the cemetery. I waited outside in front of the church.

"Crystal," I heard Dena say.

I turned around and we embraced. "Where's Sade?" I asked.

"She wanted to come, but she said she didn't think she would be able to handle it."

"I'm sure it would have been hard on her. I didn't want to be here either, but my mama made me go. Besides, JC was Ty's best friend. I wanted to come and give him moral support," I said.

"You know we need to talk. Your mom thinks you've been with me all week."

"I know. I'll tell you later." I looked around. "Now isn't the time."

"I'll hold you to it." Dena hugged me one more time before walking down the sidewalk.

The crowd finally thinned, and a long line of cars formed in front of the church and then finally proceeded toward the cemetery. I took a deep breath and burst into tears, knowing I wouldn't get to see JC's face again. Waiting for Ty at the church was best for me. I'd probably pass out, or embarrass myself by screaming at the top of my lung while seeing them put JC's body in the cold, dark ground.

Thirty-five minutes later, I heard a horn blow. I looked up and it was Ty. I rushed to get in the passenger side.

"Let's blow this joint."

I was more than ready. Ty turned the air conditioner on full blast, and we drove around for the next thirty minutes listening to one of Ty's favorite CDs. We were now driving down my street. It was hard finding a place to park.

"You sure you want to go in there?" Ty asked.

"We need to at least show our faces. And then maybe we can sneak away and go to your place," I said. "Besides, I want to get out of this dress."

Ty held his head down as we walked up the sidewalk and up the walkway. We spoke to different people as we made our way inside to a full house.

"Baby, there you are," I heard JC's mom say to Ty.

Ty said, "If you ever need any help around the house, just let me know."

"You're like my second son, so you know I will be calling you," she responded.

The woman standing in front of me now didn't act like the same grief stricken mother I'd seen earlier. Her eyes were puffy from crying, but she seemed calmer. "Come give me a hug," she said as she looked at me.

I wrapped my arms around her. She hugged me so tight that I couldn't breathe. I didn't want to say anything. It seemed like my hug was comforting to her, so I held my breath as long as I could. She released me, and I exhaled.

"Ty, I'll be right back," I said.

I went to my room to change clothes into a cool summer dress and sandals. I spent the rest of the weekend between my house and Ty's condo. I dreaded having to go home alone to my bed. Over the weekend, Ty surprised me with a teddy bear. I named it Ty and slept with it and squeezed it until I fell asleep.

The next few weeks seemed to fly by. Ty's teachers understood his situation and allowed him to take his finals, but he would have to make up for the hours during the summer. They felt sorry for him because they were under the impression that his brother was his only legal guardian.

We both crammed for final exams. Me, because I'd missed the last week of school, and him, because he'd been in and out of school for the last few months.

When the bell rang indicating it was the official last day of school, I literally skipped out of the front door. Me and the rest of the students. Ty waited for me by the curb. Some of the girls rolled their eyes as I walked by. I didn't care. They were jealous. I opened the door and threw my backpack on the backseat. I had to admit I liked the Benz better than his SUV. I leaned over and gave him a quick peck on the lips.

"I passed all of my tests," Ty said.

"Cool. So when does summer school start?" I asked.

"Next week."

"What?"

"I know. They aren't wasting any time. But it's my own fault. It's past time. I should have buckled down long before now," Ty said.

"I don't know what I'll do while you're in school," I said.

"Uh. I can think of plenty of things. You got the Summer Jam coming up."

With everything going on, I'd almost forgotten. "I came up with most of the steps, so it's not like I need to do that much rehearsing."

"Look at you. I got me a little Beyoncé on my hands."

I blushed.

"Enough about that. Let's stop and get some ice-cream and celebrate the last day of school," I said.

"Mickey D's here we come," Ty said, as he drove through the crowded streets.

FORTY-SIX

TY

To my teachers' surprise, I aced my math exams. Math had always been one of my favorite subjects. I'd always been good with numbers. I made up my mind that if things didn't work out with football, regardless, I was going to major in accounting and business. From the outside, no, I didn't look like an accountant, but that was something I wanted to do.

My doorbell rang. I wasn't expecting any company. Old habits are hard to break. I grabbed my gun, walked to the front door, and looked out the peephole. Some guy was dressed in a brown uniform holding a box. I opened the door and made sure the gun was out of sight. "May I help you?" I asked.

"Looking for a Tyreek Davis."

"Yes."

"Are you Tyreek?"

I nodded. He handed me the package and keyed in something on the device he removed from his waistline. "Have a good day."

"You too," I half-heartedly said as I shut the door.

I went to the kitchen and got a knife. I ripped the box open. Inside was a black box and a note.

You're a man now. Happy birthday.

Dad.

I couldn't help but smile, and I opened up the box. A black Rolex watch stared back at me. I removed it from the case and put it on, twisting my arm from side to side, admiring how good it looked on my wrist. I smiled. My dad hadn't forgotten. I knew then that what Michael had said two weeks ago was true. Slick was alive and well.

The doorbell rang again. I looked out the peephole. A delivery person from another carrier stood outside. Just in case it wasn't, I went to the table and picked up my gun. I opened up the door slightly. "Yes," I said when I opened the door.

"I have a package for Tyreek Davis. Just need your signature." He held a slim envelope. I signed for it, took the slim envelope, and shut the door. Frantic, I tore open the envelope. There were several sheets of paper inside. I almost missed the check that slid between the pages and hit the floor. I bent down and picked up the paper.

My eyes bucked. "Fifty thousand dollars!" I plopped down on the sofa and read over the papers. It was the money my dad had promised. The first check was fifty thousand dollars and the other money would be deposited into an account. All I needed to do was go to the bank with my check and everything would be set in motion. I would get fifty thousand dollars a month until I turned twenty-one years old, and then the remainder in one huge lump sum.

I picked up the phone to call Crystal, but put the phone down before I scrolled on her name. I wouldn't say a thing to her. Instead, there were a lot of things I needed to do between this evening and tomorrow. Tomorrow was our birthday, and I wanted to get her something real special. I'd already bought her one gift, but with fifty thousand dollars now burning a hole in my pocket, I knew the perfect gift.

Momentarily, I pushed studying aside. I grabbed my wallet, car keys, and the check, and headed straight to the bank.

I went to the bank as suggested on the papers, so I didn't have trouble opening up the account. All I did was show my ID, and I was given a new bank card and was called, "Mister Davis" with each transaction.

Yeah, boy. Money talks in this city. Now, regardless if I got a football scholarship or not, I was going to college. Besides, I really needed to take those classes because I needed to know how to handle all of my money.

I left the bank and went straight to the mall. There, I found Crystal's birthday present and let the store wrap it up. I knew she would love it. My cell phone vibrated in my pocket. "Hey, baby," I said, smiling because I had just been thinking of Crystal.

"My mom wanted to know if you liked chocolate. If so, she was going to make you a chocolate cake for the party tomorrow."

"I love chocolate. Tell her I said thank you."

"He says he loves chocolate," Crystal said to her mom.

"Baby, I'm at the store, so I'll talk to you later," I informed her.

"Getting my birthday present, I hope," she said.

"It wouldn't be a surprise if I told you. Talk to you later." I ended the call with her and walked out of the mall.

I was putting the bags in my car when I heard someone say, "Isn't that Big Mike's little brother?"

"Yeah, that's him. Let's jack that fool," the other person said.

Just when I thought life was back to normal. I really didn't want to resort to doing what I was about to do, but there was no way they were going to jack me. Not unless they were prepared to kill me.

They called themselves trying to surround me. "Hey, Doughboy. What's good?"

"Do I know you?" I asked, wishing I had my Glock on me instead of under my front seat.

"Naw, but we know your snitching brother. Because of him, my brother got arrested last week."

"I don't know nothing about that," I responded.

"You might not, but since I lost my brother, it would only be fair if he lost his too."

"Man, I ain't got no beef with either one of you. So please let me be."

"Link, he thinks we should walk away. What do you think?" the guy with the red hat on said.

"Naw, man. Look at him. Driving this Benz. Check out that wrist. Sporting a Rolex. He think he better than us. I think we need to let him know he ain't all that." He pounded his fist into the palm of his other hand.

The guy named Link grabbed me by the collar and placed his arm under my neck and threw me back up on my car. I grabbed his arm and twisted it. He shouted out in pain. His friend pulled out his gun and pointed at me. "Let him go."

"Put your weapon down and I might consider it," I said.

"I ain't putting nothing down."

I twisted the dude's arm a little more.

"Aw man. Do what he tells you," Link said.

The guy with the gun paced back and forth. From the corner of my eyes, I noticed mall security approaching. One of the security officers pointed his gun and said, "Lower your weapon."

The guy turned and aimed. The security guard opened fire. Dude fell to the ground. I pushed the guy off me whose arm I broke and raised my hands in the air. "I was getting in my car, and they tried to attack me."

The security officer patted me down. He removed my wallet and looked at my ID. "He checks out," he said to the other security officer.

I put my hands down. "Thanks. They both were trying to jack me."

"Looks like you broke one of their arms, so they both will need some medical attention."

"I need you to wait around so we can get your full statement."

"No problem." I got in my car.

An hour later, I was finally on my way home.

FORTY-SEVEN
CRYSTAL

Dear Diary,
My life has been like a whirlwind of adventure lately. There were moments I didn't know if I would be around. I haven't told my parents what happened. This is a secret Ty and I have to keep between us.

It's not every day that a girl turns sixteen. It's thirty minutes after midnight and I just talked to my boo. We've only been together a short time, but I feel like I've known Ty forever and a day. I don't know what the future holds for either one of us, but I do hope it's a future with the both of us in it together.

I finally told my girl Dena about why I used her as my alibi with my mom. She was upset but understood that the heart loves who the heart loves. She still doesn't like Ty, but that's okay. In due time, she'll grow to like him. At least I hope so. Sade's getting settled in her new place. I really like it. Sort of reminds me of Ty's.

Heard our song on the radio Friday on one of the morning shows. That's one of the best birthday presents ever. Sade says our fan pages are getting a lot of hits. I'm really excited about that.

Things with my parents have gotten a little better. My dad found a job. Talk about celebrating, that's like another early birthday gift. With him working, my mom can now stop working so many hours. I feel like I've grown up overnight. I appreciate everything my parents have done for me. One thing this situation has taught me is that even if my parents fight with each other, it doesn't mean they don't love me.

I feel like a burden's been lifted off my shoulders. I think I was putting some of the blame of their problems on me. Their issues are theirs and not mine. They will always be my parents and I will love them no matter what happens between the two of them.

My mom still wants to be the one to dress Adore. I've been outnumbered, so I had no choice but to go along with Sade and Dena's decision to allow her to do it. I just hope she doesn't have us looking like some clowns. I would hate to ruin my music career before it really got started.

Ty, oh my goodness, I love him so much. He's my everything. I know I'm only fifteen. Correction. Only sixteen, but I know the love I have for him is genuine. I know people say you're too young to be in love at my age because we don't know what love is. Well, I'm here to prove them wrong. I do know what love is and Love has one face—Ty.

I know I should be sleeping but I can't. I'm too excited about my party. My parents aren't rich, but they're still giving me a sweet sixteen party. Friends and friends of friends will all be here to wish me happy birthday.

I guess I better go so I won't wake up with bags up under my eyes as I celebrate my birthday."

I closed my diary, placed it under my pillow, and went to sleep.

The sunlight beaming through my curtains woke me out of my sound sleep. I yawned and looked at the dawn of a new day. "Good morning," I said out loud as I got out of bed.

I could hear chitter-chatter coming from down the hall and the aroma of food cooking. I went to the bathroom and showered, taking extra time getting ready. The birthday girl needed to look extra cute.

Although I dressed in a fly pair of jeans and a pink shirt, I would be wearing something different for my party. I curled my hair and put on some lip-gloss. My whole family was in the kitchen when I finally finished getting dressed.

"Good morning, birthday girl," my mama said. She hugged and kissed me.

"Happy birthday, baby girl," Dad said.

I looked in Hope's direction. "Happy birthday." She let the word 'day' drag out.

"Thanks squirt." I playfully hit her on top of the head. She blocked my hits.

I sat down at the table and enjoyed breakfast.

"I got a lot of stuff to do today to get ready for your party," my mom told me after breakfast.

"Do you need my help?" I asked, hoping she would say no because Ty had planned on taking me out to lunch since tonight we would be busy with my party.

"No, dear. I know you have plans with Ty. And no I wasn't eavesdropping on any conversations. I've been young once."

I blushed.

Two hours later, I was sitting next to Ty at our favorite restaurant, Applebees. "This is only one of your gifts," he said as he handed me the gift bag.

I took it from him and removed the paper. Inside was a red long box. I opened it up. It was a beautiful charm bracelet with several different charms on it. "This is beautiful," I said.

I handed Ty the gift bag with his gift in it. "I didn't have that much money, but I wanted to get you something that I knew you would need."

He removed the tissue paper, and I watched him remove the black leather wallet. "Thank you, baby, because the one I have is old."

Since we were seated next to each other, Ty bent over and planted a kiss on my lips. "I have another gift for you later," he said.

"Really? This is more than enough." I removed the bracelet from the box. Ty helped me put it on. I noticed for the first time, Ty's watch. I grabbed his wrist. "That's nice."

"My dad sent this to me. After the stuff that went down at the mall, I forgot to tell you," Ty said.

"Happy birthday again, Ty, and thank you for making my sixteenth birthday sweet. For a moment I thought it wouldn't be."

We ate lunch and then Ty dropped me back at home. He promised to come back later for the party. I hated to see him go. I'd planned on spending the entire evening with him, but he had one other place he wanted to go since he would be with me tonight.

FORTY-EIGHT
TY

"Look at my baby. He's not a baby anymore," my mom said, as soon as I walked in the door.

I was glad to get a call from her to let me know she was back from Louisiana.

"Mama, I'm seventeen now."

"Boy, you know I know how old you are. After being in labor with you for nine hours, I should. Just like your daddy. Big headed and stubborn."

We both laughed. She stared at my wrist. "Don't tell me. Something your dad got you. He's always been the flashy type," she said.

"Mom, I think there's something else you need to know. The condo he bought for you years ago. Well, that's where I'm staying."

"Good. Because I will never take another thing from that man."

"And Mom. If you like, I can move you out of here into a house. I have enough to put a down payment on something."

My mom put her hand up and shook her head. "Oh no, son. I took money from Michael to get this, but not my baby boy too."

"No, Mom, it's not what you think. The money is legit. Well, sort of. My daddy left me and Michael ten million dollars in the clear. I'm going to summer school, and next year I'll be a senior, and then I'm going to college."

"I don't know, Ty. Maybe you shouldn't have taken the money."

I pulled out my new wallet with my bank information. "It's all legit. It's in the bank and the money will be deposited into my account every month. When I turn twenty-one I'll be able to get the rest in bulk. By then I should be a certified accountant. Mom, I have plans."

"I see. I'm proud of you."

I laid my head on my mom's shoulder as if I was a little boy again.

"It's just the two of us, but I made you a little something," she said as she led me to the kitchen. "Happy birthday."

A cake with seventeen candles was lit up. I made a wish and blew out the candles. I thanked God for my parents, my brother, and Crystal.

"What did you wish for?" she asked.

I laughed. "Mom, you know I can't tell you. If I do, then my wish won't come true."

She hugged me. "Love you, son."

"Love you, too."

I spent the rest of the afternoon with my mom. I left her place and went home to shower and change into another outfit.

When I rolled up to Crystal's neighborhood, the party was in full swing. I knew I was a little late, but I was there and that's all that mattered. I spoke to some of the familiar faces as I walked inside in search of Crystal.

"There's the birthday boy," Crystal's mom said.

"Hi, Mrs. Maddie." She hugged me and introduced me to a few of her friends.

"Isn't he handsome?" I blushed and was finally able to ease out of the conversation and into another room.

Hope walked up to me and said, "She's still getting dressed."

"Can you tell her I'm here?" I asked.

She held out her hand. "It'll cost you."

"Pip squeak, you're always trying to milk someone out of money," I heard Dena say. She looked at me. "What's up, Ty?"

"It's all good," I responded.

"Hey, my girl told me what happened. If one hair of hers gets harmed, you'll have to deal with me. You hear me?" she lectured.

"Gotcha."

"What happened?" Hope asked.

Dena said, "Nothing. Go tell Crystal she got people waiting on her."

Hope left and about fifteen minutes later, Crystal decided to make her grand entrance. She was looking beautiful as usual. Tonight, she had an extra glow about herself. Our eyes locked. She made her way directly to me. I hugged her. "Happy birthday again," I whispered in her ear.

"Thank you, baby. And happy birthday to you too," Crystal said.

"Pictures," her mom said.

Crystal and I posed together as her dad snapped pictures. Then I stood on the sidelines as Crystal took pictures with some of her friends. Crystal motioned me to come stand by her in one of the poses with her friends. "This is Sade and her boyfriend Brandon." I recognized Sade, but never knew her name. I spoke to them both.

"Food is ready," Crystal's mom announced.

We fixed our plates and sat outside on the back where her mom had tables and chairs set up. It wasn't too hot where we couldn't enjoy being outdoors. I fanned the flies away as Crystal went from table to table talking to friends.

Crystal was definitely the star of the night, and I was proud to call her my girl.

FORTY-NINE
CRYSTAL

Dear Diary,

My sweet sixteen party was better than I could have imagined. The food was good, the presents too. I loved all of my gifts. I hung out extra long with my crew, Sade, Dena, Brandon, and my man, Ty.

Ty stayed behind after everyone left and guess what he gave me? A promise ring. It's beautiful. My mom says it looks almost like an engagement ring, but Ty assured her it was a promise ring. My dad didn't seem too happy about it, but he did agree to let me keep it. I gave him a few extra hugs.

The weeks leading up to my birthday were filled with some dangerous situations. I didn't know if I was going to come out of some of those situations alive. But as my mom would say, "Thanks to the good Lord, I'm here to write about it."

As I end this entry, I want to say the one thing I learned on turning sixteen is that nothing in this life is guaranteed. Look at my friend JC. We were the same age. I don't ever want to take things for granted. I plan on working hard and doing my best. I don't know what will happen between me and Ty in the future, but now, at this present moment, things are great. Our bond is solid. He's my soul mate. I believe that in my heart.

Tomorrow is a new day with new possibilities. As I end this last diary entry before starting a new diary, I want to say that I may complain about my parents, but I love them. Hope gets on my last nerves, but I wouldn't trade her for anything in the world. Sade and Dena will always be my girls. And Ty, well, he's my sweetheart.

I finished writing on the last page of my diary, closed it up, and locked it. It felt good to be sweet sixteen. Tomorrow, I would open up the new diary my mom got me and start a new entry. But for now, I was going to bed.

Reading Group Guide

1. Crystal was frustrated with her parents. Do you think she should have shared her feelings with her parents? Explain.

2. Do you think Crystal should have listened to Dena about Ty? Why or why not?

3. Ty seemed to be dealing with a lot of personal issues. Do you think he should have left JC and Crystal out of his mess? Explain.

4. Ty's brother, Michael, left Ty alone to fend for himself. Do you think that was right? How would you have handled the situation if you were Michael?

5. Can Ty truly turn his life around now?

6. How do you think Crystal being with Ty changed her?

7. Ty and Crystal seemed to bond due to dangerous situations. Do you think they will be happy in a drama-free environment?

8. Is sixteen too young to be in love? Explain.

9. How do you deal with your friends when they don't like the person you're dating?

10. Does the statement Tyreek's dad says, "I know what I do isn't exactly right, but I never sold drugs to anyone who didn't want them" justify anyone selling drugs? Explain.

BIO

Sparkle is the pseudonym for *Essence* Magazine bestselling author Shelia M. Goss. Besides writing young adult books, she writes books for adults. For more information,

Visit:
www.sheliagoss.com
or
www.sheliagoss.com/sparkle

You Got me Twisted

A Young Adult Novel By

GLORIA DOTSON-LEWIS

WAHIDA CLARK PRESENTS
Y.A.
YOUNG ADULT
NINETY-NINE
PROBLEMS
A Young Adult Novel BY
GLORIA DOTSON-LEWIS

WAHIDA CLARK PRESENTS
UNDER PRESSURE
Y.A.
YOUNG ADULT
A YOUNG ADULT NOVEL BY
RASHAWN HUGHES

WAHIDA CLARK PRESENTS
Y.A.
YOUNG ADULT
W·CLARK
PUBLISHING
SADE'S
SECRET
A Young Adult Novel By
SPARKLE

WAHIDA CLARK PRESENTS

Y.A.
YOUNG ADULT

THE BOY IS MINE!
A WILSON HIGH CONFIDENTIAL
A YOUNG ADULT NOVEL BY
CHARMAINE WHITE

WAHIDA CLARK PRESENTS
Y.A.
YOUNG ADULT
W·CLARK
PUBLISHING
PLAYER
HATER
A YOUNG ADULT NOVEL BY
CHARMAINE WHITE